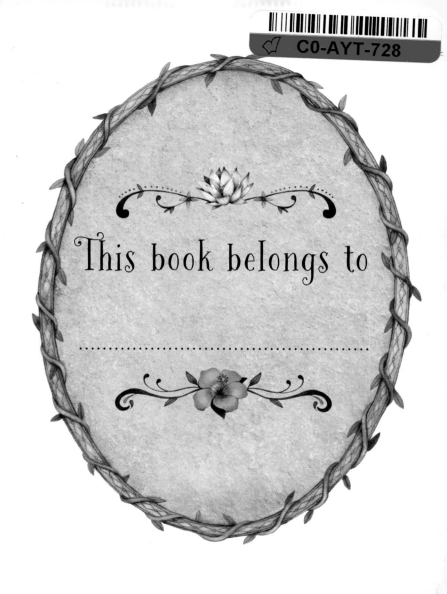

This book belongs to

. . . .

First published in 2015 by Miles Kelly Publishing Ltd
Harding's Barn, Bardfield End Green, Thaxted, Essex, CM6 3PX, UK

Copyright © Miles Kelly Publishing Ltd 2015

This edition printed 2018

2 4 6 8 10 9 7 5 3 1

Publishing Director Belinda Gallagher
Creative Director Jo Cowan
Editorial Director Rosie Neave
Senior Editor Claire Philip
Senior Designer Rob Hale
Production Elizabeth Collins, Caroline Kelly
Reprographics Stephan Davis, Jennifer Cozens, Thom Allaway
Assets Lorraine King

The publisher would like to thank Tig Thomas
for her help in compiling this book, and for
providing additional text and notes.

All rights reserved. No part of this publication may be reproduced,
stored in a retrieval system, or transmitted by any means, electronic,
mechanical, photocopying, recording or otherwise, without the prior
permission of the copyright holder.

ISBN 978-1-78617-595-3

Printed in China

British Library Cataloguing-in-Publication Data
A catalog record for this book is available from the British Library

Made with paper from a sustainable forest

www.mileskelly.net

The Jungle Book

RUDYARD
KIPLING

Illustrated by
Ester García Cortés

MILES
KELLY

Contents

Mowgli's Brothers

Now Chil the Kite brings home the night
That Mang the Bat sets free—
The herds are shut in byre and hut,
For loosed till dawn are we.
This is the hour of pride and power,
Talon and tush and claw.
Oh, hear the call! Good hunting all
That keep the Jungle Law!
NIGHT-SONG IN THE JUNGLE

T was seven o'clock of a very warm evening in the Seeonee hills when Father Wolf woke up from his day's rest, scratched himself, yawned, and spread out his paws one after the other to get rid of the sleepy feeling in their tips. Mother Wolf lay with her big grey nose dropped across her four tumbling, squealing cubs, and the moon shone into the mouth of the cave where they all lived. "*Augrh!*" said Father Wolf. "It is time to hunt again." He was going to spring downhill when a little shadow with a bushy tail crossed the threshold and whined: "Good luck go with you, O Chief of the Wolves. And good luck and strong white teeth go with noble children that they may never forget the hungry in this world."

It was the jackal – Tabaqui, the Dish-licker – and the wolves of India despise Tabaqui because he runs about making mischief, and telling tales, and eating rags and pieces of leather from the village rubbish heaps. But they are afraid of him too, because Tabaqui, more than anyone else in the jungle, is apt to go mad, and then he forgets that he was ever afraid of anyone, and runs through the forest biting everything in his way.

Even the tiger runs and hides when little Tabaqui goes mad, for madness is the most disgraceful thing that can overtake a wild creature. We call it hydrophobia, but they call it *dewanee* – the madness – and run.

"Enter, then, and look," said Father Wolf stiffly, "but there is no food here."

"For a wolf, no," said Tabaqui, "but for so mean a person as myself a dry bone is a good feast. Who are we, the *Gidur-log* [the jackal people], to pick and choose?" He scuttled to the back of the cave, where he found the bone of a buck with some meat on it, and sat cracking the end merrily.

"All thanks for this good meal," he said, licking his lips. "How beautiful are the noble children! How large are their eyes! And so young too!"

Now, Tabaqui knew as well as anyone else that there is nothing so unlucky as to compliment children to their faces. It pleased him to see Mother and Father Wolf look uncomfortable.

Tabaqui sat still, rejoicing in the mischief that he had made, and then he said spitefully:

"Shere Khan, the Big One, has shifted his

hunting grounds. He will hunt among these hills for the next moon, so he has told me."

Shere Khan was the tiger who lived near the Waingunga River, twenty miles away.

"He has no right!" Father Wolf began angrily. "By the Law of the Jungle he has no right to change without due warning. He will frighten every head of game within ten miles, and I – I have to kill for two, these days."

"His mother did not call him Lungri [the Lame One] for nothing," said Mother Wolf quietly. "He has been lame in one foot from his birth. That is why he has only killed cattle. Now the villagers of the Waingunga are angry with him, and he has come here to make our villagers angry. They will scour the jungle for him when he is far away, and we and our children must run when the grass is set alight."

"Out!" snapped Father Wolf. "Out and hunt with your master. You have done harm enough for one night."

"I go," said Tabaqui quietly. "Ye can hear Shere Khan below in the thickets. I might have saved myself the message."

Father Wolf listened, and below in the valley that ran down to a little river he heard the dry, angry, snarly, singsong whine of a tiger who has caught nothing and does not care if all the jungle knows it.

"The fool!" said Father Wolf. "To begin a night's work with that noise! Does he think that our buck are like his fat Waingunga bullocks?"

"*Hush.* It is neither bullock nor buck he hunts tonight," said Mother Wolf. "It is Man."

The whine had changed to a sort of humming purr that seemed to come from every quarter of the compass. It was the noise that bewilders woodcutters and gypsies sleeping in the open, and makes them run sometimes into the very mouth of the tiger.

"Man!" said Father Wolf, showing all his white teeth. "*Faugh!* Are there not enough beetles and frogs in the tanks that he must eat Man, and on our ground too!"

The Law of the Jungle, which never orders anything without a reason, forbids every beast to eat Man except when he is killing to show his children how to kill, and then he must hunt outside the hunting grounds of his pack or tribe. The real reason for this is that man-killing means, sooner or later, the arrival of white men on elephants, with guns, and hundreds of brown men with gongs and rockets and torches. Then everybody in the jungle suffers. The reason the beasts give among themselves is that Man is the weakest and most defenceless of all living things, and it is unsporting to touch him. They say too – and it is true – that man-eaters become mangy, and lose their teeth.

The purr grew louder, and ended in the full-throated "*Aaarh!*" of the tiger's charge.

Then there was a howl – an untigerish howl – from Shere Khan. "He has missed," said Mother Wolf. "What is it?"

Father Wolf ran out a few paces and heard Shere Khan muttering and mumbling savagely as he tumbled about in the scrub.

"The fool has had no more sense than to jump at a woodcutter's campfire, and has burned his feet," said Father Wolf with a grunt. "Tabaqui is with him."

"Something is coming uphill," said Mother

Wolf, twitching one ear. "Get ready."

The bushes rustled a little in the thicket, and Father Wolf dropped with his haunches under him, ready for his leap. Then, if you had been watching, you would have seen the most wonderful thing in the world – the wolf checked in mid-spring. He made his bound before he saw what it was he was jumping at, and then he tried to stop himself. The result was that he shot up straight into the air for four or five feet, landing almost where he left ground.

"Man!" he snapped. "A man's cub. Look!"

Directly in front of him, holding on by a low branch, stood a naked brown baby who could just walk – as soft and as dimpled a little atom as ever came to a wolf's cave at night. He looked up into Father Wolf's face, and laughed.

"Is that a man's cub?" said Mother Wolf. "I have never seen one. Bring it here."

A Wolf accustomed to moving his own cubs can, if necessary, mouth an egg without breaking it, and though Father Wolf's jaws closed right on the child's back not a tooth even scratched the skin as he laid it down among the cubs.

"How little! How naked, and – how bold!" said Mother Wolf softly. The baby was pushing his way between the cubs to get close to the warm hide. "*Ahai!* He is taking his meal with the others. And so this is a man's cub. Now, was there ever a wolf that could boast of a man's cub among her children?"

"I have heard now and again of such a thing, but never in our Pack or in my time," said Father Wolf. "He is altogether without hair, and I could kill him with a touch of my foot. But see, he looks up and is not afraid."

The moonlight was blocked out of the mouth of the cave, for Shere Khan's great square head and shoulders were thrust into the entrance. Tabaqui, behind him, was squeaking: "My lord, my lord, it went in here!"

"Shere Khan does us great honour," said Father Wolf, but his eyes were very angry. "What does Shere Khan need?"

"My quarry. A man's cub went this way," said Shere Khan. "Its parents have run off. Give it to me."

Shere Khan had jumped at a woodcutter's

campfire, as Father Wolf had said, and was furious from the pain of his burned feet. But Father Wolf knew that the mouth of the cave was too narrow for a tiger to come in by. Even where he was, Shere Khan's shoulders and forepaws were cramped for want of room, as a man's would be if he tried to fight in a barrel.

"The Wolves are a free people," said Father Wolf. "They take orders from the Head of the Pack, and not from any striped cattle-killer. The man's cub is ours – to kill if we choose."

"Ye choose and ye do not choose! What talk is this of choosing? By the bull that I killed, am I to stand nosing into your dog's den for my fair dues? It is I, Shere Khan, who speak!"

The tiger's roar filled the cave with thunder. Mother Wolf shook herself clear of the cubs and sprang forward, her eyes, like two green moons in the darkness, facing the blazing eyes of Shere Khan.

"And it is I, Raksha [The Demon], who answers. The man's cub is mine, Lungri – mine to me! He shall not be killed. He shall live to run with the Pack and to hunt with the Pack; and in the end, look you, hunter of little naked cubs – frog-eater – fish-killer – he shall hunt *you*! Now get you gone, or by the Sambhur that I killed (*I* eat no starved cattle), back you go to your mother, burned beast of the jungle, lamer than ever you came into the world! Go!"

Father Wolf looked on amazed. He had almost forgotten the days when he won Mother Wolf in fair fight from five other wolves, when she ran in the Pack and was not called The Demon for compliment's sake.

Shere Khan might have faced Father Wolf, but he could not stand up against Mother Wolf, for he knew that where he was she had all the advantage of the ground, and would fight to the death. So he backed out of the cave mouth growling, and when he was clear he shouted:

"Each dog barks in his own yard! We will see what the Pack will say to this fostering of man-cubs. The cub is mine, and to my teeth he will come in the end, O bush-tailed thieves!"

Mother Wolf threw herself down panting among the cubs, and Father Wolf said to her gravely:

"Shere Khan speaks this much truth. The cub must be shown to the Pack. Will you still keep him, Mother?"

"Keep him!" she gasped. "He came naked, by night, alone and very hungry; yet he was not afraid! Look, he has pushed one of my babes to one side already. And that lame butcher would have killed him and would have run off to the Waingunga while the villagers here hunted through all our lairs in revenge! Keep him? Assuredly I will keep him. Lie still, little frog. O you Mowgli – for Mowgli the Frog I will call you – the time will come when you will hunt Shere Khan as he has hunted you."

"But what will our Pack say?" said Father Wolf.

The Law of the Jungle lays down very clearly that any wolf may, when he marries, withdraw from the Pack he belongs to. But as soon as his cubs are old enough to stand on their feet he must bring them to the Pack Council, which is generally held once a month at full moon, in order that the other wolves may identify them. After that inspection the cubs are free to run where they please, and until they have killed their first buck no excuse is accepted if a grown wolf of the Pack kills one of them. The punishment is death where the murderer can be found; and if you think for a minute you will see that this must be so.

Father Wolf waited till his cubs could run a little, and then on the night of the Pack Meeting took them and Mowgli and Mother Wolf to the Council Rock – a hilltop covered with stones and boulders where a hundred wolves could hide. Akela, the great grey Lone Wolf, who led all the Pack by strength and cunning, lay out at full length on his rock, and below him sat forty or more wolves of every size and colour, from badger-coloured veterans who could handle a buck alone to young black three-year-olds who thought they could. The Lone Wolf had led them for a year now. He had fallen twice into a wolf trap in his youth, and once he had been beaten and left for dead; so he knew the manners and customs of men. There was very little talking at the Rock. The cubs tumbled over each other in the centre of the circle where their mothers and fathers sat, and now and again a senior wolf would go quietly up to a cub, look at him carefully, and return to his place on noiseless feet. Sometimes a mother would push her cub far out into the moonlight to be sure that he had not been overlooked. Akela from his rock would cry: "Ye know the Law – ye know the Law. Look well, O Wolves!" And the anxious mothers would take up the call: "Look – look well, O Wolves!"

At last – and Mother Wolf's neck bristles lifted as the time came – Father Wolf pushed "Mowgli the Frog," as they called him, into the centre, where he sat laughing and playing with some pebbles that glistened in the moonlight.

Akela never raised his head from his paws, but went on with the monotonous cry: "Look well!" A muffled roar came up from behind the rocks – the voice of Shere Khan crying: "The cub is mine. Give him to me. What have the Free People to do with a man's cub?" Akela never even twitched his ears. All he said was: "Look well, O Wolves! What have the Free People to do with the orders of any save the Free People? Look well!"

There was a chorus of deep growls, and a young wolf in his fourth year flung back Shere

Khan's question to Akela: "What have the Free People to do with a man's cub?" Now, the Law of the Jungle lays down that if there is any dispute as to the right of a cub to be accepted by the Pack, he must be spoken for by at least two members of the Pack who are not his father and mother.

"Who speaks for this cub?" said Akela. "Among the Free People who speaks?" There was no answer and Mother Wolf got ready for what she knew would be her last fight, if things came to fighting.

Then the only other creature who is allowed at the Pack Council – Baloo, the sleepy brown bear who teaches the wolf cubs the Law of the Jungle: old Baloo, who can come and go where he pleases because he eats only nuts and roots and honey – rose upon his hind quarters and grunted.

"The man's cub – the man's cub?" he said. "I speak for the man's cub. There is no harm in a man's cub. I have no gift of words, but I speak the truth. Let him run with the Pack, and be entered with the others. I myself will teach him."

"We need yet another," said Akela. "Baloo has

spoken, and he is our teacher for the young cubs.
Who speaks besides Baloo?"

A black shadow dropped down into the circle.
It was Bagheera the Black Panther, inky black all
over, but with the panther markings showing up
in certain lights like the pattern of watered silk.
Everybody knew Bagheera, and nobody cared to
cross his path; for he was as cunning as Tabaqui,
as bold as the wild buffalo, and as reckless as the
wounded elephant. But he had a voice as soft as
wild honey dripping from a tree, and a skin
softer than down.

"O Akela, and ye the Free People," he purred, "I
have no right in your assembly, but the Law of
the Jungle says that if there is a doubt which is
not a killing matter in regard to a new cub, the
life and safety of that cub may be bought for a
price. And the Law does not say who may or may
not pay that price. Am I right?"

"Good! Good!" said the young wolves, who are
always hungry. "Listen to Bagheera. The cub's life
can be bought for a price. It is the Law."

"Knowing that I have no right to speak here, I
ask your leave."

"Speak then," cried twenty voices.

"To kill a naked cub is shame. Besides, he may make better sport for you when he is grown. Baloo has spoken on his behalf. Now to Baloo's word I will add one bull, and a fat one, newly killed, not half a mile from here, if ye will accept the man's cub according to the Law. Is it difficult?"

There was a clamour of scores of voices, saying: "What matter? He will die in the winter rains. He will scorch in the sun. What harm can a naked frog do us? Let him run with the Pack. Where is the bull, Bagheera? Let him be accepted." And then came Akela's deep bay, crying: "Look well – look well, O Wolves!"

Mowgli was still deeply interested in the pebbles, and he did not notice when the wolves came and looked at him one by one. At last they all went down the hill for the dead bull, and only Akela, Bagheera, Baloo, and Mowgli's own wolves were left. Shere Khan roared still in the night, for he was very angry that Mowgli had not been handed over to him.

"Ay, roar well," said Bagheera, under his

whiskers, "for the time will come when this naked thing will make you roar to another tune, or I know nothing of man."

"It was well done," said Akela. "Men and their cubs are very wise. He may be a help in time."

"Truly, a help in time of need; for none can hope to lead the Pack forever," said Bagheera.

Akela said nothing. He was thinking of the time that comes to every leader of every pack when his strength goes from him and he gets feebler and feebler, till at last he is killed by the wolves and a new leader comes up – to be killed in his turn.

"Take him away," he said to Father Wolf, "and train him as befits one of the Free People."

And that is how Mowgli was entered into the Seeonee Wolf Pack for the price of a bull and on Baloo's good word.

Now you must be content to skip ten or eleven whole years, and only guess at all the wonderful life that Mowgli led among the wolves, because if it were written out it would fill ever so many books. He grew up with the cubs, though they, of course, were grown wolves almost before he was a child. And Father Wolf taught him his business, and the meaning of things in the jungle, till every rustle in the grass, every breath of the warm night air, every note of the owls above his head, every scratch of a bat's claws as it roosted for a while in a tree, and every splash of every little fish jumping in a pool meant just as much to him as the work of his office means to a business man.

When he was not learning he sat out in the sun and slept, and ate and went to sleep again. When he felt dirty or hot he swam in the forest pools; and when he wanted honey (Baloo told him that honey and nuts were just as pleasant to eat as raw meat) he climbed up for it, and that Bagheera showed him how to do.

Bagheera would lie out on a branch and call, "Come along, Little Brother," and at first Mowgli would cling like the sloth, but afterward he would fling himself through the branches almost as boldly as the grey ape. He took his place at the Council Rock, too, when the Pack met, and there he discovered that if he stared hard at any wolf, the wolf would be forced to drop his eyes, and so he used to stare for fun.

At other times he would pick the long thorns out of the pads of his friends, for wolves suffer terribly from thorns and burrs in their coats. He would go down the hillside into the cultivated lands by night, and look very curiously at the villagers in their huts, but he had a mistrust of men because Bagheera showed him a square box with a drop gate so cunningly hidden in the jungle that he nearly walked into it, and told him that it was a trap.

He loved better than anything else to go with Bagheera into the dark warm heart of the forest, to sleep all through the drowsy day, and at night see how Bagheera did his killing. Bagheera killed right and left as he felt hungry, and so did Mowgli – with one exception. As soon as he was old enough to understand things, Bagheera told him that he must never touch cattle because he had been bought into the Pack at the price of a bull's life. "All the jungle is yours," said Bagheera, "and you can kill everything that you are strong enough to kill; but for the sake of the bull that bought you, you must never kill or eat any cattle young or old. That is the Law of the Jungle." Mowgli obeyed faithfully.

And he grew and grew strong as a boy must grow who does not know that he is learning any lessons, and who has nothing in the world to think of except things to eat.

Mother Wolf told him once or twice that Shere Khan was not a creature to be trusted, and that someday he must kill Shere Khan. But though a young wolf would have remembered that advice every hour, Mowgli forgot it because he was only a boy – though he would have called himself a wolf if he had been able to speak in any human tongue.

Shere Khan was always crossing his path in the jungle, for as Akela grew older and feebler the lame tiger had come to be great friends with the younger wolves of the Pack, who followed him for scraps, a thing Akela would never have allowed if he had dared to push his authority to the proper bounds. Then Shere Khan would flatter them and wonder that such fine young hunters were content to be led by a dying wolf and a man's cub. "They tell me," Shere Khan would say, "that at Council ye dare not look him between the eyes." And the young wolves would growl and bristle.

Bagheera, who had eyes and ears everywhere, knew something of this, and once or twice he told Mowgli in so many words that Shere Khan would kill him some day. Mowgli would laugh and answer: "I have the Pack and I have you; and Baloo, though he is so lazy, might strike a blow or two for my sake. Why should I be afraid?"

It was one very warm day that a new notion came to Bagheera – born of something that he had heard. Perhaps Ikki the Porcupine had told him; but he said to Mowgli when they were deep in the jungle, as the boy lay with his head on Bagheera's beautiful black skin, "Little Brother, how often have I told you that Shere Khan is your enemy?"

"As many times as there are nuts on that palm," said Mowgli, who, naturally, could not count. "What of it? I am sleepy, Bagheera, and Shere Khan is all long tail and loud talk – like Mao, the Peacock."

"But this is no time for sleeping. Baloo knows it; I know it; the Pack know it; and even the foolish, foolish deer know. Tabaqui has told you too."

"Ho! ho!" said Mowgli. "Tabaqui came to me not long ago with some rude talk that I was a naked man's cub and not fit to dig pig-nuts. But I caught Tabaqui by the tail and swung him twice against a palm-tree to teach him better manners."

"That was foolishness, for though Tabaqui is a mischief-maker, he would have told you of something that concerned you closely. Open those eyes, Little Brother. Shere Khan dare not kill you in the jungle. But remember, Akela is very old, and soon the day will come when he cannot kill his buck, and then he will be leader no more. Many of the wolves that looked you over when you were brought to the Council first are old too, and the young wolves believe, as Shere Khan has taught them, that a man-cub has no place with the Pack. In a little time you will be a man."

"And what is a man that he should not run with his brothers?" said Mowgli. "I was born in the jungle. I have obeyed the Law of the Jungle, and there is no wolf of ours from whose paws I have not pulled a thorn. Surely they are my brothers!"

Bagheera stretched himself at full length and half shut his eyes. "Little Brother," said he, "feel under my jaw."

Mowgli put up his strong brown hand, and just under Bagheera's silky chin, where the giant rolling muscles were all hid by the glossy hair, he came upon a little bald spot.

"There is no one in the jungle that knows that I, Bagheera, carry that mark – the mark of the collar; and yet, Little Brother, I was born among men, and it was among men that my mother died – in the cages of the king's palace at Oodeypore. It was because of this that I paid the price for you at the Council when you were a little naked cub. Yes, I too was born among men. I had never seen the jungle. They fed me behind bars from an iron pan till one night I felt that I was Bagheera – the Panther – and no man's plaything, and I broke the silly lock with one blow of my paw and came away. And because I had learned the ways of men, I became more terrible in the jungle than Shere Khan. Is it not so?"

"Yes," said Mowgli, "all the jungle fear Bagheera – all except Mowgli."

"Oh, *you* are a man's cub," said the Black Panther very tenderly. "And even as I returned to my jungle, so you must go back to men at last – to the men who are your brothers – if you are not killed in the Council."

"But why – but why should any wish to kill me?" said Mowgli.

"Look at me," said Bagheera. And Mowgli looked at him steadily between the eyes. The big panther turned his head away in half a minute.

"*That* is why," he said, shifting his paw on the leaves. "Not even I can look you between the eyes, and I was born among men, and I love you, Little Brother. The others they hate you because their eyes cannot meet yours; because you are wise; because you have pulled out thorns from their feet – because you are a man."

"I did not know these things," said Mowgli sullenly, and he frowned under his heavy black eyebrows.

"What is the Law of the Jungle? Strike first and then give tongue. By your very carelessness they know that you are a man. But be wise. It is in my heart that when Akela misses his next kill – and at each hunt it costs him more to pin the buck – the Pack will turn against him and against you. They will hold a jungle Council at the Rock, and then – and then – I have it!" said Bagheera, leaping up. "Go down quickly to the men's huts in the valley, and take some of the Red Flower which they grow there, so that when the time comes you may have even a stronger friend than I or Baloo or those of the Pack that love you. Get the Red Flower."

By Red Flower Bagheera meant fire, only no creature in the jungle will call fire by its proper name. Every beast lives in deadly fear of it, and invents a hundred ways of describing it.

"The Red Flower?" said Mowgli. "That grows outside their huts in the twilight. I will get some."

"There speaks the man's cub," said Bagheera proudly. "Remember that it grows in little pots. Get one swiftly, and keep it by you for times of need."

"Good!" said Mowgli. "I go. But are you sure, O my Bagheera"– he slipped his arm around the splendid neck and looked deep into the big eyes – "are you sure that all this is Shere Khan's doing?"

"By the Broken Lock that freed me, I am sure, Little Brother."

"Then, by the Bull that bought me, I will pay Shere Khan in full for this, and maybe a little over," said Mowgli, and he bounded away.

"That is a man. That is all a man," said Bagheera to himself, lying down again. "Oh, Shere Khan, never was a blacker hunting than that frog-hunt of yours ten years ago!"

Mowgli was far and far through the forest, running hard, and his heart was hot in him. He came to the cave as the evening mist rose, and drew breath, and looked down the valley. The cubs were out, but Mother Wolf, at the back of the cave, knew by his breathing that something was troubling her frog.

"What is it, Son?" she said.

"Some bat's chatter of Shere Khan," he called back. "I hunt among the ploughed fields tonight," and he plunged downward through the bushes, to the stream at the bottom of the valley. There he checked, for he heard the yell of the Pack hunting, heard the bellow of a hunted Sambhur, and the snort as the buck turned at bay. Then there were wicked, bitter howls from the young wolves: "Akela! Akela! Let the Lone Wolf show his strength. Room for the leader of the Pack! Spring, Akela!"

The Lone Wolf must have sprung and missed his hold, for Mowgli heard the snap of his teeth and then a yelp as the Sambhur knocked him over with his forefoot.

He did not wait for anything more, but dashed on; and the yells grew fainter behind him as he ran into the croplands where the villagers lived.

"Bagheera spoke truth," he panted, as he nestled down in some cattle fodder by the window of a hut. "Tomorrow is one day both for Akela and for me."

Then he pressed his face close to the window and watched the fire on the hearth. He saw the husbandman's wife get up and feed it in the night with black lumps. And when the morning came and the mists were all white and cold, he saw the man's child pick up a wicker pot plastered inside with earth, fill it with lumps of red-hot charcoal, put it under his blanket, and go out to tend the cows in the byre.

"Is that all?" said Mowgli. "If a cub can do it, there is nothing to fear." So he strode round the corner and met the boy, took the pot from his hand, and disappeared into the mist while the boy howled with fear.

"They are very like me," said Mowgli, blowing into the pot as he had seen the woman do. "This thing will die if I do not give it things to eat," and he dropped twigs and dried bark on the red stuff. Halfway up the hill he met Bagheera with the morning dew shining like moonstones on his coat.

"Akela has missed," said the Panther. "They would have killed him last night, but they needed you also. They were looking for you on the hill."

"I was among the ploughed lands. I am ready. See!" Mowgli held up the fire pot.

"Good! Now, I have seen men thrust a dry branch into that stuff, and presently the Red Flower blossomed at the end of it. Are you not afraid?"

"No. Why should I fear? I remember now – if it is not a dream – how, before I was a Wolf, I lay beside the Red Flower, and it was warm and pleasant."

All that day Mowgli sat in the cave tending his fire pot and dipping dry branches into it to see how they looked. He found a branch that satisfied him, and in the evening when Tabaqui came to the cave and told him rudely enough that he was wanted at the Council Rock, he laughed till Tabaqui ran away. Then Mowgli went to the Council, still laughing.

Akela the Lone Wolf lay by the side of his rock as a sign that the leadership of the Pack was open, and Shere Khan, with his following of scrap-fed wolves, walked to and fro openly being flattered. Bagheera lay close to Mowgli, and the fire pot was between Mowgli's knees. When they were all gathered together, Shere Khan began to speak – a thing he would never have dared to do when Akela was in his prime.

"He has no right," whispered Bagheera. "Say so. He is a dog's son. He will be frightened."

Mowgli sprang to his feet. "Free People," he cried, "does Shere Khan lead the Pack? What has a tiger to do with our leadership?"

"Seeing that the leadership is yet open, and being asked to speak –" Shere Khan began.

"By whom?" said Mowgli. "Are we all jackals, to fawn on this cattle butcher? The leadership of the Pack is with the Pack alone."

There were yells of "Silence, you man's cub!" and "Let him speak. He has kept our Law," and at last the seniors of the Pack thundered: "Let the Dead Wolf speak." When a leader of the Pack has missed his kill, he is called the Dead Wolf as long as he lives, which is not long.

Akela raised his old head wearily:

"Free People, and ye too, jackals of Shere Khan, for twelve seasons I have led ye to and from the kill, and in all that time not one has been trapped or maimed. Now I have missed my kill. Ye know how that plot was made. Ye know how ye brought me up to an untried buck to make my weakness known. It was cleverly done. Your right is to kill me here on the Council Rock, now. Therefore, I ask, who comes to make an end of the Lone Wolf? For it is my right, by the Law of the Jungle, that ye come one by one."

There was a long hush, for no single wolf cared to fight Akela to the death. Then Shere Khan roared:

"Bah! What have we to do with this toothless fool? He is doomed to die! It is the man-cub who has lived too long. Free People, he was my meat from the first. Give him to me. He has troubled the jungle for ten seasons. Give me the man-cub, or I will hunt here always, and not give you one bone. He is a man, a man's child, and from the marrow of my bones I hate him!"

Then more than half the Pack yelled: "A man! A man! What has a man to do with us? Let him go to his own place."

"And turn all the people of the villages against us?" clamoured Shere Khan. "No, give him to me. He is a man, and none of us can look him between the eyes."

Akela lifted his head again and said, "He has eaten our food. He has slept with us. He has driven game for us. He has broken no word of the Law of the Jungle."

"Also, I paid for him with a bull when he was accepted. The worth of a bull is little, but Bagheera's honour is something that he will fight for," said Bagheera in his gentlest voice.

"A bull paid ten years ago!" the Pack snarled. "What do we care for bones ten years old?"

"Or for a pledge?" said Bagheera, his white teeth bared under his lip. "No man's cub can run with the people of the jungle," howled Shere Khan. "Give him to me!"

"He is our brother in all but blood," Akela went on, "and ye would kill him here! In truth, I have lived too long. Some of ye are eaters of cattle, and of others I have heard that, under Shere Khan's teaching, ye go by dark night and snatch children from the villagers' doorstep. Therefore I know ye to be cowards, and it is to cowards I speak. It is certain that I must die, and my life is of no worth, or I would offer that in the man-cub's place. But for the sake of the Honour of the Pack – a little matter that by being without a leader ye have forgotten – I promise that if ye let the man-cub go to his own place, I will not, when my time comes to die, bare one tooth against ye. I will die without fighting. That will at least save the Pack three lives. More I cannot do; but if ye will, I can save ye the shame that comes of killing a brother against whom there is no fault – a brother spoken for and bought into the Pack according to the Law of the Jungle."

"He is a man – a man – a man!" snarled the Pack. And most of the wolves began to gather round Shere Khan, whose tail was beginning to switch.

"Now the business is in your hands," said Bagheera to Mowgli. "*We* can do no more except fight."

Mowgli stood upright – the fire pot in his hands. Then he stretched out his arms, and yawned in the face of the Council; but he was furious with rage and sorrow, for, wolf-like, the wolves had never told him how they hated him. "Listen you!" he cried. "There is no need for this dog's jabber. Ye have told me so often tonight that I am a man (though indeed I would have been a wolf with you to my life's end) that I feel your words are true. So I do not call ye my brothers any more, but *sag* [dogs], as a man should. What ye will do, and what ye will not do, is not yours to say. That matter is with me; and that we may see the matter more plainly, I, the man, have brought here a little of the Red Flower which ye, dogs, fear."

He flung the fire pot on the ground, and some of the red coals lit a tuft of dried moss that flared up, as all the Council drew back in terror before the leaping flames.

Mowgli thrust his dead branch into the fire till the twigs lit and crackled, and whirled it above his head among the cowering wolves.

"You are the master," said Bagheera in an undertone. "Save Akela from the death. He was always your friend."

Akela, the grim old wolf who had never asked for mercy in his life, gave one piteous look at Mowgli as the boy stood all naked, his long black hair tossing over his shoulders in the light of the blazing branch that made the shadows jump and quiver.

"Good!" said Mowgli, staring round slowly. "I see that ye are dogs. I go from you to my own people – if they be my own people. The jungle is shut to me, and I must forget your talk and your companionship. But I will be more merciful than ye are. Because I was all but your brother in blood, I promise that when I am a man among men I will not betray ye to men as ye have betrayed me."

He kicked the fire with his foot, and the sparks flew up. "There shall be no war between any of us in the Pack. But here is a debt to pay before I go." He strode forward to where Shere Khan sat blinking stupidly at the flames, and caught him by the tuft on his chin. Bagheera followed in case of accidents. "Up, dog!" Mowgli cried. "Up, when a man speaks, or I will set that coat ablaze!"

Shere Khan's ears lay flat back on his head, and he shut his eyes, for the blazing branch was very near.

"This cattle-killer said he would kill me in the Council because he had not killed me when I was a cub. Thus and thus, then, do we beat dogs when we are men. Stir a whisker, Lungri, and I ram the Red Flower down your gullet!"

He beat Shere Khan over the head with the branch, and the tiger whimpered and whined in an agony of fear.

"*Pah!* Singed jungle cat – go now! But remember when next I come to the Council Rock, as a man should come, it will be with Shere Khan's hide on my head. For the rest, Akela goes free to live as he pleases. Ye will not kill him, because that is not my will. Nor do I think that ye will sit here any longer, lolling out your tongues as though ye were somebodies, instead of dogs whom I drive out – thus! Go!" The fire was burning furiously at the end of the branch, and Mowgli struck right and left round the circle, and the wolves ran howling with the sparks burning their fur. At last there were only Akela, Bagheera, and perhaps ten wolves that had taken Mowgli's part. Then something began to hurt Mowgli inside him, as he had never been hurt in his life before, and he caught his breath and sobbed, and the tears ran down his face.

"What is it? What is it?" he said. "I do not wish to leave the jungle, and I do not know what this is. Am I dying, Bagheera?"

"No, Little Brother. That is only tears," said Bagheera. "Now I know you are a man, and a man's cub no longer. Let them fall, Mowgli. They are only tears." So Mowgli sat and cried as though his heart would break; and he had never cried in all his life before.

"Now," he said, "I will go to men. But first I must say farewell to my mother." And he went to the cave where she lived with Father Wolf, and he cried on her coat, while the four cubs howled miserably.

"Ye will not forget me?" said Mowgli.

"Never while we can follow a trail," said the cubs. "Come to the foot of the hill when you are a man, and we will talk to you; and we will come into the croplands to play with you by night."

"Come soon!" said Father Wolf. "Oh, wise little frog, come again soon; for we be old, your mother and I."

"Come soon," said Mother Wolf, "little naked son of mine. For, listen, child of man, I loved you more than ever I loved my cubs."

"I will surely come," said Mowgli. "And when I come it will be to lay out Shere Khan's hide upon the Council Rock. Do not forget me! Tell them in the jungle never to forget me!"

The dawn was beginning to break when Mowgli went down the hillside alone, to meet those mysterious things that are called men.

HUNTING-SONG OF THE SEEONEE PACK

As the dawn was breaking the Sambhur belled
Once, twice and again!
And a doe leaped up, and a doe leaped up
From the pond in the wood where the wild deer sup.
This I, scouting alone, beheld,
Once, twice and again!

As the dawn was breaking the Sambhur belled
Once, twice and again!
And a wolf stole back, and a wolf stole back
To carry the word to the waiting pack,
And we sought and we found and we bayed on his track
Once, twice and again!

As the dawn was breaking the Wolf Pack yelled
Once, twice and again!
Feet in the jungle that leave no mark!
Eyes that can see in the dark – the dark!
Tongue – give tongue to it! Hark! O hark!
Once, twice and again!

Kaa's Hunting

His spots are the joy of the Leopard:
his horns are the Buffalo's pride.
Be clean, for the strength of the hunter
is known by the gloss of his hide.
If ye find that the Bullock can toss you,
or the heavy-browed Sambhur can gore;
Ye need not stop work to inform us:
we knew it ten seasons before.
Oppress not the cubs of the stranger,
but hail them as Sister and Brother,
For though they are little and fubsy, it
may be the Bear is their mother.
"There is none like to me!" says the Cub
in the pride of his earliest kill;
But the jungle is large and the Cub he is small.
Let him think and be still.

MAXIMS OF BALOO

ALL that is told here happened some time before Mowgli was turned out of the Seeonee Wolf Pack, or revenged himself on Shere Khan the tiger. It was in the days when Baloo was teaching him the Law of the Jungle. The big, serious, old brown bear was delighted to have so quick a pupil, for the young wolves will only learn as much of the Law of the Jungle as applies to their own pack and tribe, and run away as soon as they can repeat the Hunting Verse: "Feet that make no noise; eyes that can see in the dark; ears that can hear the winds in their lairs, and sharp white teeth, all these things are the marks of our brothers except Tabaqui the Jackal and the Hyena whom we hate." But Mowgli, as a man-cub, had to learn a great deal more than this. Sometimes Bagheera the Black Panther would come lounging through the jungle to see how his pet was getting on, and would purr with his head against a tree while Mowgli recited the day's lesson to Baloo. The boy could climb almost as well as he could swim, and swim almost as well as he could run. So Baloo, the Teacher of the Law, taught him the Wood and Water Laws: how to

tell a rotten branch from a sound one; how to speak politely to the wild bees when he came upon a hive of them fifty feet above ground; what to say to Mang the Bat when he disturbed him in the branches at midday; and how to warn the water snakes in the pools before he splashed down among them. None of the Jungle People like being disturbed, and all are very ready to fly at an intruder. Then, too, Mowgli was taught the Strangers' Hunting Call, which must be repeated aloud till it is answered, whenever one of the Jungle-People hunts outside his own grounds. It means, translated, "Give me leave to hunt here because I am hungry." And the answer is, "Hunt then for food, but not for pleasure."

All this will show you how much Mowgli had to learn by heart, and he grew very tired of saying the same thing over a hundred times. But as Baloo said to Bagheera one day when Mowgli had been cuffed and run off in a temper, "A man's cub is a man's cub, and he must learn all the Law of the Jungle."

"But think how small he is," said the Black Panther, who would have spoiled Mowgli if he had had his own way. "How can his little head carry all your long talk?"

"Is there anything in the jungle too little to be killed? No. That is why I teach him these things, and that is why I hit him, very softly, when he forgets."

"Softly! What do you know of softness, old Iron-feet?" Bagheera grunted. "His face is all bruised today by your – softness. *Ugh.*"

"Better he should be bruised from head to foot by me who love him than that he should come to harm through ignorance," Baloo answered very earnestly. "I am now teaching him the Master Words of the Jungle that shall protect him with the birds and the Snake People, and all that hunt on four feet, except his own pack. He can now claim protection, if he will only remember the words, from all in the jungle. Is not that worth a little beating?"

"Well, look to it then that you do not kill the man-cub. He is no tree trunk to sharpen your blunt claws upon. But what are those Master Words? I am more likely to give help than to ask it"– Bagheera stretched out one paw and admired the steel-blue, ripping-chisel talons at the end of it – "still I should like to know."

"I will call Mowgli and he shall say them – if he will. Come, Little Brother!"

"My head is ringing like a bee tree," said a sullen little voice over their heads, and Mowgli slid down a tree trunk very angry and indignant, adding as he reached the ground: "I come for Bagheera and not for *you*, fat old Baloo!"

"That is all one to me," said Baloo, though he was hurt and grieved. "Tell Bagheera, then, the Master Words of the Jungle that I have taught you this day."

"Master Words for which people?" said Mowgli, delighted to show off. "The jungle has many tongues. I know them all."

"A little you know, but not much. See, O Bagheera, they never thank their teacher. Not one small wolfling has ever come back to thank old Baloo for his teachings. Say the word for the Hunting-People, then – great scholar."

"We be of one blood, ye and I," said Mowgli, giving the words the Bear accent which all the Hunting People use.

"Good. Now for the birds."

Mowgli repeated, with the Kite's whistle at the end of the sentence.

"Now for the Snake-People," said Bagheera.

The answer was a perfectly indescribable hiss, and Mowgli kicked up his feet behind, clapped his hands together to applaud himself, and jumped on to Bagheera's back, where he sat sideways, drumming with his heels on the glossy skin and making the worst faces he could think of at Baloo.

"There – there! That was worth a little bruise," said the brown bear tenderly. "Someday you will remember me." Then he turned aside to tell Bagheera how he had begged the Master Words from Hathi the Wild Elephant, who knows all about these things, and how Hathi had taken Mowgli down to a pool to get the Snake Word from a water snake, because Baloo could not pronounce it, and how Mowgli was now reasonably safe against all accidents in the jungle, because neither snake, bird, nor beast would hurt him.

"No one then is to be feared," Baloo wound up,

patting his big furry stomach with pride.

"Except his own tribe," said Bagheera, under his breath; and then aloud to Mowgli, "Have a care for my ribs, Little Brother! What is all this dancing up and down?"

Mowgli had been trying to make himself heard by pulling at Bagheera's shoulder fur and kicking hard. When the two listened to him he was shouting at the top of his voice, "And so I shall have a tribe of my own, and lead them through the branches all day long."

"What is this new foolishness, little dreamer of dreams?" said Bagheera.

"Yes, and throw branches and dirt at old Baloo," Mowgli went on. "They have promised me this. Ah!"

"*Whoof!*" Baloo's big paw scooped Mowgli off Bagheera's back, and as the boy lay between the big fore-paws he could see the Bear was angry.

"Mowgli," said Baloo, "you have been talking with the *Bandar-log* – the Monkey People."

Mowgli looked at Bagheera to see if the Panther was angry too, and Bagheera's eyes were as hard as jade stones.

"You have been with the Monkey People – the grey apes – the people without a law – the eaters of everything. That is great shame."

"When Baloo hurt my head," said Mowgli (he was still on his back), "I went away, and the grey apes came down from the trees and had pity on me. No one else cared." He snuffled a little.

"The pity of the Monkey People!" Baloo snorted. "The stillness of the mountain stream! The cool of the summer sun! And then, man-cub?"

"And then, and then, they gave me nuts and pleasant things to eat, and they – they carried me in their arms up to the top of the trees and said I was their blood brother except that I had no tail, and should be their leader someday."

"They have no leader," said Bagheera. "They lie. They have always lied."

"They were very kind and told me to come again. Why have I never been taken among the Monkey People? They stand on their feet as I do. They do not hit me with their hard paws. They play all day. Let me get up! Bad Baloo, let me up! I will play with them again."

"Listen, man-cub," said the Bear, and his voice rumbled like thunder on a hot night. "I have taught you all the Law of the Jungle for all the peoples of the jungle – except the Monkey-Folk who live in the trees. They have no law. They are outcasts. They have no speech of their own, but use the stolen words which they overhear when they listen, and peep, and wait up above in the branches. Their way is not our way. They are without leaders. They have no remembrance. They boast and chatter and pretend that they are a great people about to do great affairs in the jungle, but the falling of a nut turns their minds to laughter and all is forgotten. We of the jungle have no dealings with them. We do not drink where the monkeys drink; we do not go where the monkeys go; we do not hunt where they hunt; we do not die where they die. Have you ever heard me speak of the *Bandar-log* till today?"

"No," said Mowgli in a whisper, for the forest was very still now Baloo had finished.

"The Jungle-People put them out of their mouths and out of their minds. They are very many, evil, dirty, shameless, and they desire, if they have any fixed desire, to be noticed by the Jungle People. But we do not notice them even when they throw nuts and filth on our heads."

He had hardly spoken when a shower of nuts and twigs spattered down through the branches; and they could hear coughings and howlings and angry jumpings high up in the air among the thin branches.

"The Monkey-People are forbidden," said Baloo, "forbidden to the Jungle-People. Remember."

"Forbidden," said Bagheera, "but I still think Baloo should have warned you against them."

"I – I? How was I to guess he would play with such dirt. The Monkey People! *Faugh!*"

A fresh shower came down on their heads and the two trotted away, taking Mowgli with them. What Baloo had said about the monkeys was perfectly true. They belonged to the treetops, and as beasts very seldom look up, there was no occasion for the monkeys and the Jungle-People to cross each other's path. But whenever they found a sick wolf, or a wounded tiger, or bear, the monkeys would torment him, and would throw sticks and nuts at any beast for fun and in the hope of being noticed. Then they would howl and shriek senseless songs, and invite the Jungle-People to climb up their trees and fight them, or would start furious battles over nothing among themselves, and leave the dead monkeys where the Jungle-People could see them. They were always just going to have a leader, and laws and customs of their own, but they never did, because their memories would not hold over from day to day, and so they compromised things by making up a saying, "What the *Bandar-log* think now the jungle will think later," and that comforted them a great deal. None of the beasts could reach them, but on the other hand none of the beasts would notice them, and that was why they were so pleased when Mowgli came to play with them, and they heard how angry Baloo was.

They never meant to do any more – the *Bandar-log* never mean anything at all; but one of them invented what seemed to him a brilliant idea, and he told all the others that Mowgli would be a useful person to keep in the tribe, because he could weave sticks together for protection from the wind; so, if they caught him, they could make him teach them. Of course Mowgli, as a woodcutter's child, inherited all sorts of instincts, and used to make little huts of fallen branches without thinking how he came to do it. The Monkey-People, watching in the trees, considered his play most wonderful. This time, they said, they were really going to have a leader and become the wisest people in the jungle – so wise that everyone else would notice and envy them. Therefore they followed Baloo and Bagheera and Mowgli through the jungle very quietly till it was time for the midday nap, and Mowgli, who was very much ashamed of himself, slept between the Panther and the Bear, resolving to have no more to do with the Monkey People.

The next thing he remembered was feeling hands on his legs and arms – hard, strong, little hands – and then a swash of branches in his face, and then he was staring down through the swaying boughs as Baloo woke the jungle with his deep cries and Bagheera bounded up the trunk with every tooth bared. The *Bandar-log* howled with triumph and scuffled away to the

upper branches where Bagheera dared not follow,
shouting: "He has noticed us! Bagheera has
noticed us. All the Jungle-People admire us for
our skill and our cunning." Then they began their
flight; and the flight of the Monkey-People
through tree-land is one of the things nobody can
describe. They have their regular roads and
crossroads, up hills and down hills, all laid out
from fifty to seventy or a hundred feet above
ground, and by these they can travel even at night
if necessary. Two of the strongest monkeys caught
Mowgli under the arms and swung off with him
through the treetops, twenty feet at a bound. Had
they been alone they could have gone twice as
fast, but the boy's weight held them back. Sick
and giddy as Mowgli was he could not help
enjoying the wild rush, though the glimpses of
earth far down below frightened him, and the
terrible check and jerk at the end of the swing
over nothing but empty air brought his heart
between his teeth. His escort would rush him up
a tree till he felt the thinnest topmost branches
crackle and bend under them, and then with a
cough and a whoop would fling themselves into

the air outward and downward, and bring up, hanging by their hands or their feet to the lower limbs of the next tree. Sometimes he could see for miles and miles across the still green jungle, as a man on the top of a mast can see for miles across the sea, and then the branches and leaves would lash him across the face, and he and his two guards would be almost down to earth again. So, bounding and crashing and whooping and yelling, the whole tribe of *Bandar-log* swept along the tree roads with Mowgli their prisoner.

For a time he was afraid of being dropped. Then he grew angry but knew better than to struggle, and then he began to think. The first thing was to send back word to Baloo and Bagheera, for, at the pace the monkeys were going, he knew his friends would be left far behind. It was useless to look down, for he could only see the topsides of the branches, so he stared upward and saw, far away in the blue, Chil the Kite balancing and wheeling as he kept watch over the jungle waiting for things to die. Chil saw that the monkeys were carrying something, and dropped a few hundred yards to find out whether their load was good to eat. He whistled with surprise when he saw Mowgli being dragged up to a treetop and heard him give the Kite call for – "We be of one blood, you and I." The waves of the branches closed over the boy, but Chil balanced away to the next tree in time to see the little brown face come up again. "Mark my trail!" Mowgli shouted. "Tell Baloo of the Seeonee Pack and Bagheera of the Council Rock."

"In whose name, Brother?" Chil had never seen Mowgli before, though of course he had heard of him.

"Mowgli, the Frog. Man-cub they call me! Mark my trail!"

The last words were shrieked as he was being swung through the air, but Chil nodded and rose up till he looked no bigger than a speck of dust, and there he hung, watching with his telescope eyes the swaying of the treetops as Mowgli's escort whirled along.

"They never go far," he said with a chuckle. "They never do what they set out to do. Always pecking at new things are the *Bandar-log*. This time, if I have any eyesight, they have pecked down trouble for themselves, for Baloo is no fledgling and Bagheera can, as I know, kill more than goats."

So he rocked on his wings, his feet gathered up under him, and waited.

Meantime, Baloo and Bagheera were furious with rage and grief. Bagheera climbed as he had never climbed before, but the thin branches broke beneath his weight, and he slipped down, his claws full of bark.

"Why did you not warn the man-cub?" he roared to poor Baloo, who had set off at a clumsy trot in the hope of overtaking the monkeys. "What was the use of half slaying him with blows if you did not warn him?"

"Haste! O haste! We – we may catch them yet!" Baloo panted.

"At that speed! It would not tire a wounded cow. Teacher of the Law – cub-beater – a mile of that rolling to and fro would burst you open. Sit still and think! Make a plan. This is no time for chasing. They may drop him if we follow too close."

"*Arrula! Whoo!* They may have dropped him

already, being tired of carrying him. Who can trust the *Bandar-log*? Put dead bats on my head! Give me black bones to eat! Roll me into the hives of the wild bees so that I may be stung to death, and bury me with the Hyena, for I am most miserable of bears! *Arulala! Wahooa!* O Mowgli, Mowgli! Why did I not warn you against the Monkey-Folk instead of smacking your head? Now perhaps I may have knocked the day's lesson out of his mind, and he will be alone in the jungle without the Master Words."

Baloo clasped his paws over his ears and rolled to and fro moaning.

"At least he gave me all the Words correctly a little time ago," said Bagheera impatiently. "Baloo, you have neither memory nor respect. What would the jungle think if I, the Black Panther, curled myself up like Ikki the Porcupine, and howled?"

"What do I care what the jungle thinks? He may be dead by now."

"Unless and until they drop him from the branches in sport, or kill him out of idleness, I have no fear for the man-cub. He is wise and well taught, and above all he has the eyes that make the Jungle-People afraid. But (and it is a great evil) he is in the power of the *Bandar-log*, and they, because they live in trees, have no fear of any of our people." Bagheera licked one forepaw thoughtfully.

"Fool that I am! Oh, fat, brown, root-digging fool that I am," said Baloo, uncoiling himself with a jerk, "it is true what Hathi the Wild Elephant says: *'To each his own fear'*; and they, the *Bandar-log*, fear Kaa the Rock Snake. He can climb as well as they can. He steals the young monkeys in the night. The whisper of his name makes their wicked tails cold. Let us go to Kaa."

"What will he do for us? He is not of our tribe, being footless – and with most evil eyes," said Bagheera.

"He is very old and very cunning. Above all, he is always hungry," said Baloo hopefully. "Promise him many goats."

"He sleeps for a full month after he has once eaten. He may be asleep now, and even if he were awake what if he would rather kill his own goats?" Bagheera, who did not know much about

Kaa, was naturally suspicious.

"Then in that case, you and I together, old hunter, might make him see reason." Here Baloo rubbed his faded brown shoulder against the Panther, and they went off to look for Kaa the Rock Python.

They found him stretched out on a warm ledge in the afternoon sun, admiring his beautiful new coat, for he had been in retirement for the last ten days changing his skin, and now he was very splendid – darting his big blunt-nosed head along the ground, and twisting the thirty feet of his body into fantastic knots and curves, and licking his lips as he thought of his dinner to come.

"He has not eaten," said Baloo, with a grunt of relief, as soon as he saw the beautifully mottled brown and yellow jacket. "Be careful, Bagheera! He is always a little blind after he has changed his skin, and very quick to strike."

Kaa was not a poison snake – in fact he rather despised the poison snakes as cowards – but his strength lay in his hug, and when he had once lapped his huge coils round anybody there was no more to be said. "Good hunting!" cried Baloo, sitting up on his haunches. Like all snakes of his breed Kaa was rather deaf, and did not hear the call at first. Then he curled up ready for any accident, his head lowered.

"Good hunting for us all," he answered. "Oho, Baloo, what do you do here? Good hunting, Bagheera. One of us at least needs food. Is there any news of game afoot? A doe now, or even a young buck? I am as empty as a dried well."

"We are hunting," said Baloo carelessly. He knew that you must not hurry Kaa. He is too big.

"Give me permission to come with you," said Kaa. "A blow more or less is nothing to you, Bagheera or Baloo, but I – I have to wait and wait for days in a wood path and climb half a night on the mere chance of a young ape. Psshaw! The branches are not what they were when I was young. Rotten twigs and dry boughs are they all."

"Maybe your great weight has something to do with the matter," said Baloo.

"I am a fair length – a fair length," said Kaa with a little pride. "But for all that, it is the fault of this new-grown timber. I came very near to

falling on my last hunt – very near indeed – and the noise of my slipping, for my tail was not tight wrapped around the tree, woke the *Bandar-log*, and they called me most evil names."

"Footless, yellow earth-worm," said Bagheera under his whiskers, as though he were trying to remember something.

"*Sssss!* Have they ever called me *that*?" said Kaa.

"Something of that kind it was that they shouted to us last moon, but we never noticed them. They will say anything – even that you have lost all your teeth, and will not face anything bigger than a kid, because (they are indeed shameless, these *Bandar-log*) – because you are afraid of the he-goat's horns," Bagheera went on sweetly.

Now a snake, especially a wary old python like Kaa, very seldom shows that he is angry, but Baloo and Bagheera could see the big swallowing muscles on either side of Kaa's throat ripple and bulge.

"The *Bandar-log* have shifted their grounds," he said quietly. "When I came up into the sun today I heard them whooping among the treetops."

"It – it is the *Bandar-log* that we follow now," said Baloo, but the words stuck in his throat, for that was the first time in his memory that one of the Jungle-People had admitted to being interested in the doings of the monkeys.

"Beyond doubt then it is no small thing that takes two such hunters – leaders in their own jungle I am certain – on the trail of the *Bandar-log*," Kaa replied courteously, as he swelled with curiosity.

"Indeed," Baloo began, "I am no more than the old and sometimes very foolish Teacher of the Law to the Seeonee wolf-cubs, and Bagheera here –"

"Is Bagheera," said the Black Panther, and his jaws shut with a snap, for he did not believe in being humble. "The trouble is this, Kaa. Those nut-stealers and pickers of palm leaves have stolen away our man-cub of whom you have perhaps heard."

"I heard some news from Ikki of a man-thing that was part of a wolf pack, but I did not believe. Ikki is full of stories half heard and very badly told."

"But it is true. He is such a man-cub as never was," said Baloo. "The best and wisest and boldest of man-cubs – my own pupil, who shall make the name of Baloo famous through all the jungles; and besides, I – we – love him, Kaa."

"*Ts! Ts!*" said Kaa, weaving his head to and fro. "I also have known what love is. There are tales I could tell that –"

"That need a clear night when we are all well fed to praise properly," said Bagheera quickly. "Our man-cub is in the hands of the *Bandar-log* now, and we know that of all the Jungle-People they fear Kaa alone."

"They fear me alone. They have good reason," said Kaa. "Chattering, foolish, vain – vain, foolish, and chattering, are the monkeys. But a man-thing in their hands is in no good luck. They grow tired of the nuts they pick, and throw them down. They carry a branch half a day, meaning to do great things with it, and then they snap it in two. That man-thing is not to be envied. They called me also – 'yellow fish' was it not?"

"Worm – worm – earth-worm," said Bagheera, "as well as other things which I cannot now say for shame."

"We must remind them to speak well of their master. *Aaa-ssp!* We must help their wandering memories. Now, where did they go with the cub?"

"The jungle alone knows. Toward the sunset, I believe," said Baloo. "We thought that you would know, Kaa."

"I? How? I take them when they come in my way, but I do not hunt the *Bandar-log*, or frogs – or green scum on a water-hole, for that matter."

"Up, Up! Up, Up! Hillo! Illo! Illo, look up, Baloo of the Seeonee Wolf Pack!"

Baloo looked up to see where the voice came from, and there was Chil the Kite, sweeping down with the sun shining on the upturned flanges of his wings. It was near Chil's bedtime, but he had ranged all over the jungle looking for the Bear and had missed him in the thick foliage.

"What is it?" said Baloo.

"I have seen Mowgli among the *Bandar-log*. He told me to tell you. I watched. The *Bandar-log* have taken him beyond the river to the monkey city – to the Cold Lairs. They may stay there for a night, or ten nights, or an hour. I have told the bats to watch through the dark time. That is my message. Good hunting, all you below!"

"Full gorge and a deep sleep to you, Chil," cried Bagheera. "I will remember you in my next kill, and put aside the head for you alone, O best of kites!"

"It is nothing. It is nothing. The boy held the Master Word. I could have done no less," and Chil circled up again to his roost.

"He has not forgotten to use his tongue," said Baloo with a chuckle of pride. "To think of one so young remembering the Master Word for the birds too while he was being pulled across trees!"

"It was most firmly driven into him," said Bagheera. "But I am proud of him, and now we must go to the Cold Lairs."

They all knew where that place was, but few of the Jungle People ever went there, because what they called the Cold Lairs was an old deserted city, lost and buried in the jungle, and beasts seldom use a place that men have once used. The wild boar will, but the hunting tribes do not. Besides, the monkeys lived there as much as they could be said to live anywhere, and no self-respecting animal would come within eyeshot of it except in times of drought, when the half-ruined tanks and reservoirs held a little water.

"It is half a night's journey – at full speed," said Bagheera, and Baloo looked very serious. "I will go as fast as I can," he said anxiously.

"We dare not wait for you. Follow, Baloo. We must go on the quick-foot – Kaa and I."

"Feet or no feet, I can keep abreast of all your four," said Kaa shortly. Baloo made one effort to hurry, but had to sit down panting, and so they left him to come on later, while Bagheera hurried forward, at the quick panther-canter. Kaa said nothing, but, strive as Bagheera might, the huge Rock-python held level with him. When they came to a hill stream, Bagheera gained, because he bounded across while Kaa swam, his head and two feet of his neck clearing the water, but on level ground Kaa made up the distance.

"By the Broken Lock that freed me," said Bagheera, when twilight had fallen, "You are no slow goer!"

"I am hungry," said Kaa. "Besides, they called me speckled frog."

"Worm – earth-worm, and yellow to boot."

"All one. Let us go on," and Kaa seemed to pour himself along the ground, finding the shortest road with his steady eyes, and keeping to it.

In the Cold Lairs the Monkey-People were not thinking of Mowgli's friends at all. They had brought the boy to the Lost City, and were very much pleased with themselves for the time. Mowgli had never seen an Indian city before, and though this was almost a heap of ruins it seemed very wonderful and splendid. Some king had built it long ago on a little hill. You could still trace the stone causeways that led up to the ruined gates where the last splinters of wood hung to the worn, rusted hinges. Trees had grown into and out of the walls; the battlements were tumbled down and decayed, and wild creepers hung out of the windows of the towers on the walls in bushy hanging clumps.

A great roofless palace crowned the hill, and the marble of the courtyards and the fountains was split, and stained with red and green, and the very cobblestones in the courtyard where the king's elephants used to live had been thrust up and apart by grasses and young trees. From the palace you could see the rows and rows of roofless houses that made up the city looking like empty honeycombs filled with blackness; the shapeless block of stone that had been an idol in the square where four roads met; the pits and dimples at street corners where the public wells once stood, and the shattered domes of temples with wild figs sprouting on their sides. The monkeys called the place their city, and pretended to despise the Jungle-People because they lived in the forest. And yet they never knew what the buildings were made for nor how to use them. They would sit in circles on the hall of the king's council chamber, and scratch for fleas and pretend to be men; or they would run in and out of the roofless houses and collect pieces of plaster and old bricks in a corner, and forget where they had hidden them, and fight and cry in scuffling crowds, and then break off to play up and down the terraces of the king's garden, where they would shake the rose trees and the oranges in sport to see the fruit and flowers fall. They explored all the passages and dark tunnels in the palace and the hundreds of little dark rooms, but they never remembered what they had seen and what they had not; and so drifted about in ones and twos or crowds telling each other that they were doing as men did. They drank at the tanks and made the water all muddy, and then they fought over it, and then they would all rush together in mobs and shout: "There is no one in the jungle so wise and good and clever and strong and gentle as the *Bandar-log*." Then all would begin again till they grew tired of the city and went back to the treetops, hoping the Jungle-People would notice them.

Mowgli, who had been trained under the Law of the Jungle, did not like or understand this kind of life. The monkeys dragged him into the Cold Lairs late in the afternoon, and instead of going to sleep, as Mowgli would have done after a long journey, they joined hands and danced about and sang their foolish songs. One of the monkeys made a speech and told his companions that Mowgli's capture marked a new thing in the history of the *Bandar-log*, for Mowgli was going to show them how to weave sticks and canes

together as a protection against rain and cold. Mowgli picked up some creepers and began to work them in and out, and the monkeys tried to imitate; but in a very few minutes they lost interest and began to pull their friends' tails or jump up and down on all fours, coughing.

"I wish to eat," said Mowgli. "I am a stranger in this part of the jungle. Bring me food, or give me leave to hunt here."

Twenty or thirty monkeys bounded away to bring him nuts and wild pawpaws. But they fell to fighting on the road, and it was too much trouble to go back with what was left of the fruit. Mowgli was sore and angry as well as hungry, and he roamed through the empty city giving the Strangers' Hunting Call from time to time, but no one answered him, and Mowgli felt that he had reached a very bad place indeed. "All that Baloo has said about the *Bandar-log* is true," he thought to himself. "They have no Law, no Hunting Call, and no leaders – nothing but foolish words and little picking thievish hands. So if I am starved or killed here, it will be all my own fault. But I must try to return to my own jungle. Baloo will surely beat me, but that is better than chasing silly rose leaves with the *Bandar-log*."

No sooner had he walked to the city wall than the monkeys pulled him back, telling him that he did not know how happy he was, and pinching him to make him grateful. He set his teeth and said nothing, but went with the shouting monkeys to a terrace above the red sandstone reservoirs that were half-full of rain water. There was a ruined summerhouse of white marble in the centre of the terrace, built for queens dead a hundred years ago. The domed roof had half fallen in and blocked up the underground passage from the palace by which the queens used to enter. But the walls were made of screens of marble tracery – beautiful milk-white fretwork, set with agates and cornelians and jasper and lapis lazuli, and as the moon came up behind the hill it shone through the open work, casting shadows on the ground like black velvet embroidery. Sore, sleepy, and hungry as he was, Mowgli could not help laughing when the *Bandar-log* began, twenty at a time, to tell him how great and wise and strong and gentle they were, and how foolish he was to wish to leave them. "We are great. We are free. We are wonderful. We are the most wonderful people in all the jungle! We all say so, and so it must be true," they shouted. "Now as you are a new listener and can carry our words back to the Jungle-People so that they may notice us in future, we will tell you all about our most excellent selves." Mowgli made no objection, and the monkeys gathered by hundreds and hundreds on the terrace to listen to their own speakers singing the praises of the *Bandar-log*, and whenever a speaker stopped for want of breath they would all shout together: "This is true; we all say so." Mowgli nodded and blinked, and said "Yes" when they asked him a question, and his head spun with the noise. "Tabaqui the Jackal must have bitten all these people," he said to himself, "and now they have madness. Certainly this is *dewanee*, the madness. Do they never go to sleep? Now there is a cloud coming to cover that moon. If it were only a big enough cloud I might try to run away in the darkness. But I am tired."

That same cloud was being watched by two

good friends in the ruined ditch below the city wall, for Bagheera and Kaa, knowing well how dangerous the Monkey-People were in large numbers, did not wish to run any risks. The monkeys never fight unless they are a hundred to one, and few in the jungle care for those odds.

"I will go to the west wall," Kaa whispered, "and come down swiftly with the slope of the ground in my favour. They will not throw themselves upon *my* back in their hundreds, but – "

"I know it," said Bagheera. "I wish that Baloo were here, but we must do what we can. When that cloud covers the moon I shall go to the terrace. They hold some sort of council there over the boy."

"Good hunting," said Kaa grimly, and glided away to the west wall. That happened to be the least ruined of any, and the big snake was delayed awhile before he could find a way up the stones. The cloud hid the moon, and as Mowgli wondered what would come next he heard Bagheera's light feet on the terrace. The Black Panther had raced up the slope almost without a sound and was striking – he knew better than to

waste time in biting – right and left among the
monkeys, who were seated round Mowgli in
circles fifty and sixty deep. There was a howl of
fright and rage, and then as Bagheera tripped on
the rolling kicking bodies beneath him, a monkey
shouted: "There is only one here! Kill him! Kill."
A scuffling mass of monkeys, biting, scratching,
tearing, and pulling, closed over Bagheera, while
five or six laid hold of Mowgli, dragged him
up the wall of the summerhouse and pushed him
through the hole of the broken dome. A man-
trained boy would have been badly bruised,
for the fall was a good fifteen feet, but Mowgli
fell as Baloo had taught him to fall, and landed
on his feet.

"Stay there," shouted the monkeys, "till we have
killed your friends, and later we will play with
you – if the Poison-People leave you alive."

"We be of one blood, ye and I," said Mowgli,
quickly giving the Snake's Call. He could hear
rustling and hissing in the rubbish all round him
and gave the Call a second time, to make sure.

"Even ssso! Down hoods all!" said half a dozen
low voices (every ruin in India becomes sooner

or later a dwelling place of snakes, and the old summerhouse was alive with cobras). "Stand still, Little Brother, for your feet may do us harm."

Mowgli stood as quietly as he could, peering through the open work and listening to the furious din of the fight round the Black Panther – the yells and chatterings and scufflings, and Bagheera's deep, hoarse cough as he backed and bucked and twisted and plunged under the heaps of his enemies. For the first time since he was born, Bagheera was fighting for his life.

"Baloo must be at hand; Bagheera would not have come alone," Mowgli thought. And then he called aloud: "To the tank, Bagheera. Roll to the water tanks. Roll and plunge! Get to the water!"

Bagheera heard, and the cry that told him Mowgli was safe gave him new courage. He worked his way desperately, inch by inch, straight for the reservoirs, halting in silence. Then from the ruined wall nearest the jungle rose up the rumbling war-shout of Baloo. The old Bear had done his best, but he could not come before. "Bagheera," he shouted, "I am here. I climb! I haste! *Ahuwora!* The stones slip under my feet! Wait my

coming, O most infamous *Bandar-log*!" He panted
up the terrace only to disappear to the head in a
wave of monkeys, but he threw himself squarely
on his haunches, and, spreading out his forepaws,
hugged as many as he could hold, and then began
to hit with a regular bat – bat – bat, like the
flipping strokes of a paddle wheel. A crash and a
splash told Mowgli that Bagheera had fought his
way to the tank where the monkeys could not
follow. The Panther lay gasping for breath, his
head just out of the water, while the monkeys
stood three deep on the red steps, dancing up and
down with rage, ready to spring upon him from
all sides if he came out to help Baloo. It was then
that Bagheera lifted up his dripping chin, and in
despair gave the Snake's Call for protection – "We
be of one blood, ye and I" – for he believed that
Kaa had turned tail at the last minute. Even
Baloo, half smothered under the monkeys on the
edge of the terrace, could not help chuckling as
he heard the Black Panther asking for help.

Kaa had only just worked his way over the
west wall, landing with a wrench that dislodged a
coping stone into the ditch. He had no intention

of losing any advantage of the ground, and coiled and uncoiled himself once or twice, to be sure that every foot of his long body was in working order. All that while the fight with Baloo went on, and the monkeys yelled in the tank round Bagheera, and Mang the Bat, flying to and fro, carried the news of the great battle over the jungle, till even Hathi the Wild Elephant trumpeted, and, far away, scattered bands of the Monkey-Folk woke and came leaping along the tree-roads to help their comrades in the Cold Lairs, and the noise of the fight roused all the day birds for miles round. Then Kaa came straight, quickly, and anxious to kill. The fighting strength of a python is in the driving blow of his head backed by all the strength and weight of his body. If you can imagine a lance, or a battering ram, or a hammer weighing nearly half a ton driven by a cool, quiet mind living in the handle of it, you can roughly imagine what Kaa was like when he fought. A python four or five feet long can knock a man down if he hits him fairly in the chest, and Kaa was thirty feet long, as you know. His first stroke was delivered into the heart of the crowd round Baloo. It was sent home with shut mouth in silence, and there was no need of a second. The monkeys scattered with cries of – "Kaa! It is Kaa! Run! Run!"

Generations of monkeys had been scared into good behaviour by the stories their elders told them of Kaa, the night thief, who could slip along the branches as quietly as moss grows, and steal away the strongest monkey that ever lived; of old Kaa, who could make himself look so like a dead branch or a rotten stump that the wisest were deceived, till the branch caught them. Kaa was everything that the monkeys feared in the jungle, for none of them knew the limits of his power, none of them could look him in the face, and none had ever come alive out of his hug. And so they ran, stammering with terror, to the walls and the roofs of the houses, and Baloo drew a deep breath of relief. His fur was much thicker than Bagheera's, but he had suffered sorely in the fight. Then Kaa opened his mouth for the first time and spoke one long hissing word, and the faraway monkeys, hurrying to the defence of the Cold Lairs, stayed where they were, cowering, till the loaded branches bent and crackled under them. The monkeys on the walls and the empty houses stopped their cries, and in the stillness that fell upon the city Mowgli heard Bagheera shaking his wet sides as he came up from the tank. Then the clamour broke out again. The monkeys leaped higher up the walls. They clung around the necks of the big stone idols and shrieked as they skipped along the battlements, while Mowgli, in the summerhouse, put his eye to the screenwork and hooted owl-fashion between his front teeth, to show his derision and contempt.

"Get the man-cub out of that trap; I can do no more," Bagheera gasped. "Let us take the man-cub and go. They may attack again."

"They will not move till I order them. Stay you sssso!" Kaa hissed, and the city was silent once more. "I could not come before, Brother, but I *think* I heard you call,"– this was to Bagheera.

"I – I may have cried out in the battle," Bagheera answered. "Baloo, are you hurt?

"I am not sure that they did not pull me into a hundred little bearlings," said Baloo, gravely shaking one leg after the other. "*Wow!* I am sore. Kaa, we owe you, I think, our lives – Bagheera and I."

"No matter. Where is the manling?"

"Here, in a trap. I cannot climb out," cried Mowgli. The curve of the broken dome was above his head.

"Take him away. He dances like Mao the Peacock. He will crush our young," said the cobras inside.

"Hah!" said Kaa with a chuckle, "he has friends everywhere, this manling. Stand back, manling. And hide you, O Poison People. I break down the wall."

Kaa looked carefully till he found a discoloured crack in the marble tracery showing a weak spot, made two or three light taps with his head to get the distance, and then lifting up six feet of his body clear of the ground, sent home half a dozen full-power smashing blows, nose first. The screen-work broke and fell away in a cloud of dust and rubbish, and Mowgli leaped through the opening and flung himself between Baloo and Bagheera – an arm around each big neck.

"Are you hurt?" said Baloo, hugging him softly.

"I am sore, hungry, and not a little bruised. But, oh, they have treated you badly, my Brothers! Ye bleed."

"Others also," said Bagheera, licking his lips and looking at the monkey-dead on the terrace and round the tank.

"It is nothing, it is nothing, if you are safe, oh, my pride of all little frogs!" whimpered Baloo.

"Of that we shall judge later," said Bagheera, in a dry voice that Mowgli did not at all like. "But here is Kaa to whom we owe the battle and you owe your life. Thank him according to our customs, Mowgli."

Mowgli turned and saw the great Python's head swaying a foot above his own.

"So this is the manling," said Kaa. "Very soft is his skin, and he is not unlike the *Bandar-log*. Take care, manling, that I do not mistake you for a monkey some twilight when I have newly changed my coat."

"We be one blood, you and I," Mowgli answered. "I take my life from you tonight. My kill shall be your kill if ever you are hungry, O Kaa."

"All thanks, Little Brother," said Kaa, though his eyes twinkled. "And what may so bold a hunter kill? I ask so that I may follow when next he goes hunting."

"I kill nothing – I am too little – but I drive goats toward such as can use them. When you are empty come to me and see if I speak the truth. I have some skill in these [he held out his hands], and if ever you are in a trap, I may pay the debt which I owe to you, to Bagheera, and to Baloo, here. Good hunting to ye all, my masters."

"Well said," growled Baloo, for Mowgli had returned thanks very prettily. The Python dropped his head lightly for a minute on Mowgli's shoulder. "A brave heart and a courteous tongue," said he. "They shall carry you far through the jungle, manling. But now go hence quickly with your friends. Go and sleep, for the moon sets, and what follows it is not good that you should see."

The moon was sinking behind the hills and the lines of trembling monkeys huddled together on the walls and battlements looked like ragged shaky fringes of things. Baloo went down to the tank for a drink and Bagheera began to put his fur in order, as Kaa glided out into the centre of the terrace and brought his jaws together with a ringing snap that drew all the monkeys' eyes upon him.

"The moon sets," he said. "Is there yet light enough to see?"

From the walls came a moan like the wind in the treetops – "We see, O Kaa."

"Good. Now begins the dance – the Dance of the Hunger of Kaa. Sit still and watch."

He turned twice or thrice in a big circle, weaving his head from right to left. Then he began making loops and figures of eight with his body, and soft, oozy triangles that melted into squares and five-sided figures, and coiled mounds, never resting, never hurrying, and never stopping his low humming song. It grew darker and darker, till at last the dragging, shifting coils disappeared, but they could hear the rustle of the scales.

Baloo and Bagheera stood still as stone, growling in their throats, their neck hair bristling, and Mowgli watched and wondered.

"*Bandar-log*," said the voice of Kaa at last, "can ye stir foot or hand without my order? Speak!"

"Without your order we cannot stir foot or hand, O Kaa!"

"Good! Come all one pace nearer to me."

The lines of the monkeys swayed forward helplessly, and Baloo and Bagheera took one stiff step forward with them.

"Nearer!" hissed Kaa, and they all moved again.

Mowgli laid his hands on Baloo and Bagheera to get them away, and the two great beasts jumped as though they had been woken from a dream.

"Keep your hand on my shoulder," Bagheera whispered. "Keep it there, or I must go back – must go back to Kaa. Aah!"

"It is only old Kaa making circles on the dust," said Mowgli. "Let us go." And the three slipped off through a gap in the walls to the jungle.

"*Whoof!*" said Baloo, when he stood under the still trees again. "Never more will I make an ally of Kaa," and he shook himself all over.

"He knows more than we," said Bagheera,

trembling. "In a little time, had I stayed, I should have walked down his throat."

"Many will walk by that road before the moon rises again," said Baloo. "He will have good hunting – after his own style."

"But what was the meaning of it all?" said Mowgli, who did not know anything of a python's powers of hypnotism. "I saw no more than a big snake making foolish circles till the dark came. And his nose was all sore. Ho! Ho!"

"Mowgli," said Bagheera angrily, "his nose was sore on your account, as my ears and sides and paws, and Baloo's neck and shoulders are bitten on your account. Neither Baloo nor Bagheera will be able to hunt with pleasure for many days."

"It is nothing," said Baloo; "we have the man-cub again."

"True, but he has cost us heavily in time which might have been spent in good hunting, in wounds, in hair – I am half plucked along my back – and last of all, in honour. For, remember, Mowgli, I, who am the Black Panther, was forced to call upon Kaa for protection, and Baloo and I were both made stupid as little birds by the

Hunger Dance. All this, man-cub, came of your playing with the *Bandar-log*."

"True, it is true," said Mowgli sorrowfully. "I am an evil man-cub, and my stomach is sad in me."

"*Mf!* What says the Law of the Jungle, Baloo?"

Baloo did not wish to bring Mowgli into any more trouble, but he could not tamper with the Law, so he mumbled: "Sorrow never prevents punishment. But remember, Bagheera, he is very little."

"I will remember. But he has done mischief, and blows must be dealt now. Mowgli, have you anything to say?"

"Nothing. I did wrong. Baloo and you are wounded. It is just."

Bagheera gave him half a dozen love-taps from a panther's point of view (they would hardly have waked one of his own cubs), but for a seven-year-old boy they amounted to as severe a beating as you could wish to avoid. When it was all over Mowgli sneezed, and picked himself up without a word.

"Now," said Bagheera, "jump on my back, Little Brother, and we will go home."

One of the beauties of Jungle Law is that punishment settles all scores. There is no nagging afterward.

Mowgli laid his head down on Bagheera's back and slept so deeply that he never woke when he was put down in the home cave.

ROAD-SONG OF THE BANDAR-LOG

Here we go in a flung festoon,
Halfway up to the jealous moon!
Don't you envy our pranceful bands?
Don't you wish you had extra hands?
Wouldn't you like if your tails were – so –
Curved in the shape of a Cupid's bow?
Now you're angry, but – never mind,
Brother, your tail hangs down behind!

Here we sit in a branchy row,
Thinking of beautiful things we know;
Dreaming of deeds that we mean to do,
All complete, in a minute or two –
Something noble and wise and good,
Done by merely wishing we could.
We've forgotten, but – never mind,
Brother, your tail hangs down behind!

All the talk we ever have heard
Uttered by bat or beast or bird –
Hide or fin or scale or feather –
Jabber it quickly and all together!
Excellent! Wonderful! Once again!
Now we are talking just like men!
Let's pretend we are ... never mind,
Brother, your tail hangs down behind!
This is the way of the Monkey-kind.

Then join our leaping lines that scumfish
through the pines,
That rocket by where, light and high,
the wild grape swings.
By the rubbish in our wake, and the
noble noise we make,
Be sure, be sure, we're going to do some
splendid things!

"Tiger! Tiger!"

What of the hunting, hunter bold?
Brother, the watch was long and cold.
What of the quarry ye went to kill?
Brother, he crops in the jungle still.
Where is the power that made your pride?
Brother, it ebbs from my flank and side.
Where is the haste that ye hurry by?
Brother, I go to my lair – to die.

Now we must go back to the first tale. When Mowgli left the wolf's cave after the fight with the Pack at the Council Rock, he went down to the ploughed lands where the villagers lived, but he would not stop there because it was too near to the jungle, and he knew that he had made at least one bad enemy at the Council. So he hurried on, keeping to the rough road that ran down the valley, and followed it at a steady jog-trot for nearly twenty miles, till he came to a country that he did not know. The valley opened out into a great plain dotted over with rocks and cut up by ravines. At one end stood a little village, and at the other the thick jungle came down in a sweep to the grazing-grounds, and stopped there as though it had been cut off with a hoe. All over the plain, cattle and buffaloes were grazing, and when the little boys in charge of the herds saw Mowgli they shouted and ran away, and the yellow dogs that hang about every Indian village barked. Mowgli walked on, for he was feeling hungry, and when he came to the village gate he saw the big thornbush that was drawn up before the gate at twilight, pushed to one side.

"*Umph!*" he said, for he had come across more than one such barricade in his night rambles after things to eat. "So men are afraid of the People of the Jungle here also." He sat down by the gate, and when a man came out he stood up, opened his mouth, and pointed down it to show that he wanted food. The man stared, and ran back up the one street of the village shouting for the priest, who was a big, fat man dressed in white, with a red and yellow mark on his forehead. The priest came to the gate, and with him at least a hundred people, who stared and talked and shouted and pointed at Mowgli.

"They have no manners, these Men Folk," said Mowgli to himself. "Only the grey ape would behave as they do." So he threw back his long hair and frowned at the crowd.

"What is there to be afraid of?" said the priest. "Look at the marks on his arms and legs. They are the bites of wolves. He is but a wolf child run away from the jungle."

Of course, in playing together, the cubs had often nipped Mowgli harder than they intended, and there were white scars all over his arms and legs. But he would have been the last person in the world to call these bites, for he knew what real biting meant.

"*Arré! Arré!*" said two or three women together. "To be bitten by wolves, poor child! He is a handsome boy. He has eyes like red fire. By my honour, Messua, he is not unlike your boy that was taken by the tiger."

"Let me look," said a woman with heavy copper rings on her wrists and ankles, and she peered at Mowgli under the palm of her hand. "Indeed he is. He is thinner, but he has the very look of my boy."

The priest was a clever man, and he knew that Messua was wife to the richest villager in the place. So he looked up at the sky for a minute and said solemnly: "What the jungle has taken the jungle has restored. Take the boy into your house, my sister, and forget not to honour the priest who sees so far into the lives of men."

"By the Bull that bought me," said Mowgli to himself, "but all this talking is like another looking-over by the Pack! Well, if I am a man, a man I must become."

The crowd parted as the woman beckoned Mowgli to her hut, where there was a red lacquered bedstead, a great earthen grain chest with funny raised patterns on it, half a dozen copper cooking pots, an image of a Hindu god in a little alcove, and on the wall a real mirror, such as they sell at the country fairs.

She gave him a long drink of milk and some bread, and then she laid her hand on his head and looked into his eyes; for she thought perhaps that he might be her real son come back from the jungle where the tiger had taken him. So she said, "Nathoo, O Nathoo!" Mowgli did not show that he knew the name. "Do you not remember the day when I gave you your new shoes?" She touched his foot, and it was almost as hard as horn. "No," she said sorrowfully, "those feet have never worn shoes, but you are very like my Nathoo, and you shall be my son."

Mowgli was uneasy, because he had never been under a roof before. But as he looked at the thatch, he saw that he could tear it out any time if he wanted to get away, and that the window had no fastenings. "What is the good of a man," he said to himself at last, "if he does not understand man's talk? Now I am as silly and dumb as a man would be with us in the jungle. I must speak their talk."

It was not for fun that he had learned while he was with the wolves to imitate the challenge of bucks in the jungle and the grunt of the little wild pig. So, as soon as Messua pronounced a word Mowgli would imitate it almost perfectly, and before dark he had learned the names of many things in the hut.

There was a difficulty at bedtime, because Mowgli would not sleep under anything that looked so like a panther trap as that hut, and when they shut the door he went through the window. "Give him his will," said Messua's husband. "Remember he can never till now have slept on a bed. If he is indeed sent in the place of our son he will not run away."

So Mowgli stretched himself in some long, clean grass at the edge of the field, but before he had closed his eyes a soft grey nose poked him under the chin.

"*Phew!*" said Grey Brother (he was the eldest of

Mother Wolf's cubs). "This is a poor reward for
following you twenty miles. You smell of wood
smoke and cattle – altogether like a man already.
Wake, Little Brother; I bring news."

"Are all well in the jungle?" said Mowgli,
hugging him.

"All except the wolves that were burned with
the Red Flower. Now, listen. Shere Khan has gone
away to hunt far off till his coat grows again, for
he is badly singed. When he returns he swears
that he will lay your bones in the Waingunga."

"There are two words to that. I also have made
a little promise. But news is always good. I am
tired tonight – very tired with new things, Grey
Brother – but bring me the news always."

"You will not forget that you are a wolf? Men
will not make you forget?" said Grey Brother
anxiously.

"Never. I will always remember that I love you
and all in our cave. But also I will always
remember that I have been cast out of the Pack."

"And that you may be cast out of another pack.
Men are only men, Little Brother, and their talk is
like the talk of frogs in a pond. When I come

down here again, I will wait for you in the bamboos at the edge of the grazing-ground."

For three months after that night Mowgli hardly ever left the village gate, he was so busy learning the ways and customs of men. First he had to wear a cloth round him, which annoyed him horribly; and then he had to learn about money, which he did not in the least understand, and about ploughing, of which he did not see the use. Then the little children in the village made him very angry. Luckily, the Law of the Jungle had taught him to keep his temper, for in the jungle life and food depend on keeping your temper; but when they made fun of him because he would not play games or fly kites, or because he mispronounced some word, only the knowledge that it was wrong to kill little naked cubs kept him from picking them up and breaking them in two.

He did not know his own strength in the least. In the jungle he knew he was weak compared with the beasts, but in the village people said that he was as strong as a bull.

And Mowgli had not the faintest idea of the

difference that caste makes between man and man. When the potter's donkey slipped in the clay pit, Mowgli hauled it out by the tail, and helped to stack the pots for their journey to the market at Khanhiwara. That was very shocking, too, for the potter is a low-caste man, and his donkey is worse. When the priest scolded him, Mowgli threatened to put him on the donkey too, and the priest told Messua's husband that Mowgli had better be set to work as soon as possible; and the village headman told Mowgli that he would have to go out with the buffaloes next day, and herd them while they grazed. No one was more pleased than Mowgli; and that night, because he had been appointed a servant of the village, as it were, he went off to a circle that met every evening on a masonry platform under a great fig-tree. It was the village club, and the headman and the watchman and the barber, who knew all the gossip of the village, and old Buldeo, the village hunter, who had a musket, met and smoked. The monkeys sat and talked in the upper branches, and there was a hole under the platform where a cobra lived, and he had his little platter of milk every night because he was sacred; and the old men sat around the tree and talked, and pulled at the big *huqas* (the water-pipes) till far into the night. They told wonderful tales of gods and men and ghosts; and Buldeo told even more wonderful ones of the ways of beasts in the jungle, till the eyes of the children sitting outside the circle bulged out of their heads. Most of the tales were about animals, for the jungle was always at their door. The deer and the wild pig grubbed up their crops, and now and again the tiger carried off a man at twilight, within sight of the village gates.

Mowgli, who naturally knew something about what they were talking of, had to cover his face not to show that he was laughing, while Buldeo, the musket across his knees, climbed on from one wonderful story to another, and Mowgli's shoulders shook.

Buldeo was explaining how the tiger that had carried away Messua's son was a ghost tiger, and his body was inhabited by the ghost of a wicked, old moneylender, who had died some years ago. "And I know that this is true," he said, "because

Purun Dass always limped from the blow that he got in a riot when his account books were burned, and the tiger that I speak of limps, too, for the tracks of his pads are unequal."

"True, true, that must be the truth," said the grey-beards, nodding together.

"Are all these tales such cobwebs and moon talk?" said Mowgli. "That tiger limps because he was born lame, as everyone knows. To talk of the soul of a moneylender in a beast that never had the courage of a jackal is child's talk."

Buldeo was speechless with surprise for a moment, and the headman stared.

"Oho! It is the jungle brat, is it?" said Buldeo. "If you are so wise, better bring his hide to Khanhiwara, for the Government has set a hundred rupees on his life. Better still, talk not when your elders speak."

Mowgli rose to go. "All the evening I have lain here listening," he called back over his shoulder, "and, except once or twice, Buldeo has not said one word of truth concerning the jungle, which is at his very doors. How, then, shall I believe the tales of ghosts and gods and goblins which he says he has seen?"

"It is full time that boy went to herding," said the headman, while Buldeo puffed and snorted at Mowgli's impertinence.

The custom of most Indian villages is for a few boys to take the cattle and buffaloes out to graze in the early morning, and bring them back at night. The very cattle that would trample a white man to death allow themselves to be banged and bullied and shouted at by children that hardly come up to their noses. So long as the boys keep with the herds they are safe, for not even the tiger will charge a mob of cattle. But if they straggle to pick flowers or hunt lizards, they are sometimes carried off. Mowgli went through the village street in the dawn, sitting on the back of Rama, the great herd bull. The slaty-blue buffaloes, with their long, backward-sweeping horns and savage eyes, rose out their byres, one by one, and followed him, and Mowgli made it very clear to the children with him that he was the master. He beat the buffaloes with a long, polished bamboo, and told Kamya, one of the boys, to graze the cattle by themselves, while he went on with the buffaloes, and to be very careful not to stray away from the herd.

An Indian grazing ground is all rocks and scrub and tussocks and little ravines, among which the herds scatter and disappear. The buffaloes generally keep to the pools and muddy places, where they lie wallowing or basking in the warm mud for hours. Mowgli drove them on to the edge of the plain where the Waingunga came out of the jungle; then he dropped from Rama's neck, trotted off to a bamboo clump, and found Grey Brother. "Ah," said Grey Brother, "I have waited here very many days. What is the meaning of this cattle-herding work?"

"It is an order," said Mowgli. "I am a village herd for a while. What news of Shere Khan?"

"He has come back to this country, and has waited here a long time for you. Now he has gone off again, for the game is scarce. But he means to kill you."

"Very good," said Mowgli. "So long as he is away let you or one of the four brothers sit on that rock, so that I can see you as I come out of the village. When he comes back wait for me in the

ravine by the *dhák* tree in the centre of the plain.
We need not walk into Shere Khan's mouth."

Then Mowgli picked out a shady place, and lay
down and slept while the buffaloes grazed round
him. Herding in India is one of the laziest things
in the world. The cattle move and crunch, and lie
down, and move on again, and they do not even
low. They only grunt, and the buffaloes very
seldom say anything, but get down into the
muddy pools one after another, and work their
way into the mud till only their noses and staring
china-blue eyes show above the surface, and then
they lie like logs. The sun makes the rocks dance
in the heat, and the herd children hear one kite
(never any more) whistling almost out of sight
overhead, and they know that if they died, or a
cow died, that kite would sweep down, and the
next kite miles away would see him drop and
follow, and the next, and the next, and almost
before they were dead there would be a score of
hungry kites come out of nowhere. Then they
sleep and wake and sleep again, and weave little
baskets of dried grass and put grasshoppers in
them; or catch two praying mantises and make

them fight; or string a necklace of red and black
jungle nuts; or watch a lizard basking on a rock,
or a snake hunting a frog near the wallows. Then
they sing long, long songs with odd quavers at the
end of them, and the day seems longer than most
people's whole lives, and perhaps they make a
mud castle with mud figures of men and horses
and buffaloes, and put reeds into the men's
hands, and pretend that they are kings and the
figures are their armies, or that they are gods to
be worshipped. Then evening comes and the
children call, and the buffaloes lumber up out of
the sticky mud with noises like gunshots going
off one after the other, and they all string across
the grey plain back to the twinkling village lights.

Day after day Mowgli would lead the buffaloes
out to their wallows, and day after day he would
see Grey Brother's back a mile and a half away
across the plain (so he knew that Shere Khan had
not come back), and day after day he would lie
on the grass listening to the noises round him,
and dreaming of old days in the jungle. If Shere
Khan had made a false step with his lame paw up
in the jungles by the Waingunga, Mowgli would

have heard him in those long, still mornings.

At last a day came when he did not see Grey
Brother at the signal place, and he laughed and
headed the buffaloes for the ravine by the *dhák*
tree, which was all covered with golden-red
flowers. There sat Grey Brother, every bristle on
his back lifted.

"He has hidden for a month to throw you off
your guard. He crossed the ranges last night with
Tabaqui, hot-foot on your trail," said the Wolf,
panting.

Mowgli frowned. "I am not afraid of Shere
Khan, but Tabaqui is very cunning."

"Have no fear," said Grey Brother, licking his
lips a little. "I met Tabaqui in the dawn. Now he
is telling all his wisdom to the kites, but he told
me everything before I broke his back. Shere
Khan's plan is to wait for you at the village gate
this evening – for you and for no one else. He is
lying up now, in the big dry ravine of the
Waingunga."

"Has he eaten today, or does he hunt empty?"
said Mowgli, for the answer meant life and death
to him.

"He killed at dawn, – a pig, – and he has drunk too. Remember, Shere Khan could never fast, even for the sake of revenge."

"Oh! Fool, fool! What a cub's cub it is! Eaten and drunk too, and he thinks that I shall wait till he has slept! Now, where does he lie up? If there were but ten of us we might pull him down as he lies. These buffaloes will not charge unless they wind him, and I cannot speak their language. Can we get behind his track so that they may smell it?"

"He swam far down the Waingunga to cut that off," said Grey Brother.

"Tabaqui told him that, I know. He would never have thought of it alone." Mowgli stood with his finger in his mouth, thinking. "The big ravine of the Waingunga. That opens out on the plain not half a mile from here. I can take the herd round through the jungle to the head of the ravine and then sweep down – but he would slink out at the foot. We must block that end. Grey Brother, can you cut the herd in two for me?"

"Not I, perhaps – but I have brought a wise helper." Grey Brother trotted off and dropped

into a hole. Then there lifted up a huge grey head
that Mowgli knew well, and the hot air was filled
with the most desolate cry of all the jungle – the
hunting howl of a wolf at midday.

"Akela! Akela!" said Mowgli, clapping his hands.
"I might have known that you would not forget
me. We have a big work in hand. Cut the herd in
two, Akela. Keep the cows and calves together,
and the bulls and the plough buffaloes by
themselves."

The two wolves ran in and out of the herd,
which snorted and threw up its head, and
separated into two clumps. In one, the cow-
buffaloes stood with their calves in the centre,
and glared and pawed, ready, if a wolf would only
stay still, to charge down and trample the life out
of him. In the other, the bulls and the young bulls
snorted and stamped, but though they looked
more imposing they were much less dangerous,
for they had no calves to protect. No six men
could have divided the herd so neatly.

"What orders!" panted Akela. "They are trying
to join again."

Mowgli slipped on to Rama's back. "Drive the

bulls away to the left, Akela. Grey Brother, when we are gone, hold the cows together, and drive them into the foot of the ravine."

"How far?" said Grey Brother, panting and snapping.

"Till the sides are higher than Shere Khan can jump," shouted Mowgli. "Keep them there till we come down." The bulls swept off as Akela bayed, and Grey Brother stopped in front of the cows. They charged down on him, and he ran just before them to the foot of the ravine, as Akela drove the bulls far to the left.

"Well done! Another charge and they are fairly started. Careful, now – careful, Akela. A snap too much and the bulls will charge. *Hujah!* This is wilder work than driving black buck. Did you think these creatures could move so swiftly?" Mowgli called.

"I have – have hunted these too in my time," gasped Akela in the dust. "Shall I turn them into the jungle?"

"Ay! Turn. Swiftly turn them! Rama is mad with rage. Oh, if I could only tell him what I need of him today."

The bulls were turned, to the right this time, and crashed into the standing thicket. The other herd children, watching with the cattle half a mile away, hurried to the village as fast as their legs could carry them, crying that the buffaloes had gone mad and run away.

But Mowgli's plan was simple enough. All he wanted to do was to make a big circle uphill and get at the head of the ravine, and then take the bulls down it and catch Shere Khan between the bulls and the cows; for he knew that after a meal and a full drink Shere Khan would not be in any condition to fight or to clamber up the sides of the ravine. He was soothing the buffaloes now by voice, and Akela had dropped far to the rear, only whimpering once or twice to hurry the rearguard. It was a long, long circle, for they did not wish to get too near the ravine and give Shere Khan warning. At last Mowgli rounded up the bewildered herd at the head of the ravine on a grassy patch that sloped steeply down to the ravine itself. From that height you could see across the tops of the trees down to the plain below; but what Mowgli looked at was the sides of the ravine, and he saw with a great deal of satisfaction that they ran nearly straight up and down, while the vines and creepers that hung over them would give no foothold to a tiger who wanted to get out.

"Let them breathe, Akela," he said, holding up his hand. "They have not smelt him yet. Let them breathe. I must tell Shere Khan who comes. We have him in the trap."

He put his hands to his mouth and shouted down the ravine – it was almost like shouting down a tunnel – and the echoes jumped from rock to rock.

After a long time there came back the drawling, sleepy snarl of a full-fed tiger just wakened.

"Who calls?" said Shere Khan, and a splendid peacock fluttered up out of the ravine screeching.

"I, Mowgli. Cattle thief, it is time to come to the Council Rock! Down – hurry them down, Akela! Down, Rama, down!"

The herd paused for an instant at the edge of the slope, but Akela gave tongue in the full hunting yell, and they pitched over one after the other, just as steamers shoot rapids, the sand and stones spurting up round them. Once started, there was no chance of stopping, and before they were in the bed of the ravine Rama smelt Shere Khan and bellowed.

"Ha! Ha!" said Mowgli, on his back. "Now you know!" and the torrent of black horns, foaming muzzles, and staring eyes whirled down the ravine just as boulders go down in floodtime; the weaker buffaloes being shouldered out to the sides of the ravine where they tore through the creepers. They knew what the business was before them – the terrible charge of the buffalo herd against which no tiger can hope to stand. Shere Khan heard the thunder of their hoofs, picked himself up, and lumbered down the ravine, looking from side to side for some way of escape, but the walls of the ravine were straight and he had to hold on, heavy with his dinner and his drink, willing to do anything rather than fight. The herd splashed through the pool he had just left, bellowing till the narrow cut rang. Mowgli heard an answering bellow from the foot of the ravine, saw Shere Khan turn (the tiger

knew if the worst came to the worst it was better to meet the bulls than the cows with their calves), and then Rama tripped, stumbled, and went on again over something soft, and, with the bulls at his heels, crashed full into the other herd, while the weaker buffaloes were lifted clean off their feet by the shock of the meeting. That charge carried both herds out into the plain, goring and stamping and snorting. Mowgli watched his time, and slipped off Rama's neck, laying about him right and left with his stick.

"Quick, Akela! Break them up. Scatter them, or they will be fighting one another. Drive them away, Akela. *Hai,* Rama! *Hai, hai, hai* my children! Softly now, softly! It is all over."

Akela and Grey Brother ran to and fro nipping the buffaloes' legs, and though the herd wheeled once to charge up the ravine again, Mowgli managed to turn Rama, and the others followed him to the wallows.

Shere Khan needed no more trampling. He was dead, and the kites were coming for him already.

"Brothers, that was a dog's death," said Mowgli, feeling for the knife he carried in a sheath round his neck now that he lived with men. "But he would never have shown fight. *Wallah!* His hide will look well on the Council Rock. We must get to work swiftly."

A boy trained among men would never have dreamed of skinning a ten-foot tiger alone, but Mowgli knew better than anyone else how an animal's skin is fitted on, and how it can be taken off. But it was hard work, and Mowgli slashed and tore and grunted for an hour, while the wolves lolled out their tongues, or came forward and tugged as he ordered them. Presently a hand fell on his shoulder, and looking up he saw Buldeo with the Tower musket. The children had told the village about the buffalo stampede, and Buldeo went out angrily, only too anxious to correct Mowgli for not taking better care of the herd. The wolves dropped out of sight as soon as they saw the man coming.

"What is this foolishness?" said Buldeo angrily. "To think that you can skin a tiger! Where did the buffaloes kill him? It is the Lame Tiger too, and there is a hundred rupees on his head. Well, well, we will overlook your letting the herd run off, and perhaps I will give you one of the rupees of the reward when I have taken the skin to Khanhiwara." He fumbled in his waist cloth for flint and steel, and stooped down to singe Shere Khan's whiskers. Most Indian hunters always singe a tiger's whiskers to prevent his ghost from haunting them.

"*Hum!*" said Mowgli, half to himself as he ripped back the skin of a forepaw. "So you will take the hide to Khanhiwara for the reward, and perhaps give me one rupee? Now it is in my mind that I need the skin for my own use. *Heh!* Old man, take away that fire!"

"What talk is this to the chief hunter of the village? Your luck and the stupidity of your buffaloes have helped you to this kill. The tiger had just fed, or he would have gone twenty miles by this time. You cannot even skin him properly, little beggar brat, and then I, Buldeo, must be told not to singe his whiskers. Mowgli, I will not give you one coin of the reward, but only a very big beating. Leave the carcass!"

"By the Bull that bought me," said Mowgli, who was trying to get at the shoulder, "must I stay babbling to an old ape all noon? Here, Akela, this man plagues me."

Buldeo, who was still stooping over Shere Khan's head, found himself sprawling on the grass, with a grey wolf standing over him, while Mowgli went on skinning as though he were alone in all India.

"Ye – es," he said, between his teeth. "You are altogether right, Buldeo. You will never give me one coin of the reward. There is an old war between this lame tiger and myself – a very old war, and – I have won."

To do Buldeo justice, if he had been ten years younger he would have taken his chance with Akela had he met the wolf in the woods, but a wolf who obeyed the orders of this boy who had private wars with man-eating tigers was not a common animal. It was sorcery, magic of the worst kind, thought Buldeo, and he wondered whether the charm round his neck would protect him. He lay as still as still, expecting every minute to see Mowgli turn into a tiger too.

"Maharaj! Great King," he said at last in a husky whisper.

"Yes," said Mowgli, without turning his head, chuckling a little.

"I am an old man. I did not know that you were anything more than a herdsboy. May I rise up and go away, or will your servant tear me to pieces?"

"Go, and peace go with you. Only, another time do not meddle with my game. Let him go, Akela."

Buldeo hobbled away to the village as fast as he could, looking back over his shoulder in case Mowgli should change into something terrible. When he got to the village he told a tale of magic and enchantment and sorcery that made the priest look very serious.

Mowgli went on with his work, but it was nearly twilight before he and the wolves had drawn the great striped skin clear of the body.

"Now we must hide this and take the buffaloes home! Help me to herd them, Akela."

The herd rounded up in the misty twilight, and when they got near the village Mowgli saw lights, and heard the conches and bells in the temple blowing and banging. Half the village seemed to be waiting for him by the gate. "That is because I have killed Shere Khan," he said to himself. But a shower of stones whistled about his ears, and the villagers shouted: "Sorcerer! Wolf's brat! Jungle demon! Go away! Get gone quickly or the priest will turn you into a wolf again. Shoot, Buldeo, shoot!"

The old musket went off with a bang, and a young buffalo bellowed in pain.

"More sorcery!" shouted the villagers. "He can turn bullets. Buldeo, that was *your* buffalo."

"Now what is this?" said Mowgli, bewildered, as the stones flew thicker.

"They are not unlike the Pack, these brothers of yours," said Akela, sitting down composedly. "It is in my head that, if bullets mean anything, they would cast you out."

"Wolf! Wolf's cub! Go away!" shouted the priest, waving a sprig of the sacred *tulsi* plant.

"Again? Last time it was because I was a man. This time it is because I am a wolf. Let us go, Akela."

A woman – it was Messua – ran across to the herd, and cried: "Oh, my son, my son! They say you are a sorcerer who can turn himself into a beast at will. I do not believe it, but go away or they will kill you. Buldeo says you are a wizard, but I know you have avenged Nathoo's death."

"Come back, Messua!" shouted the crowd. "Come back, or we will stone you."

Mowgli laughed a little short ugly laugh, for a stone had hit him in the mouth. "Run back, Messua. This is one of the foolish tales they tell under the big tree at dusk. I have at least paid for your son's life. Farewell; and run quickly, for I shall send the herd in more swiftly than their stones. I am no wizard, Messua. Farewell!"

"Now, once more, Akela," he cried. "Bring the herd in."

The buffaloes were anxious enough to get to the village. They hardly needed Akela's yell, but charged through the gate like a whirlwind, scattering the crowd right and left.

"Keep count!" shouted Mowgli scornfully. "It may be that I have stolen one of them. Keep count, for I will do your herding no more. Fare you well, children of men, and thank Messua that I do not come in with my wolves and hunt you up and down your street."

He turned on his heel and walked away with the Lone Wolf, and as he looked up at the stars he felt happy. "No more sleeping in traps for me, Akela. Let us get Shere Khan's skin and go away. No, we will not hurt the village, for Messua was kind to me."

When the moon rose over the plain, making it look all milky, the horrified villagers saw Mowgli, with two wolves at his heels and a bundle on his head, trotting across at the steady wolf's trot that eats up the long miles like fire. Then they banged the temple bells and blew the conches louder than ever. And Messua cried, and Buldeo told and retold the story of his adventures in the jungle, till he ended by saying that Akela stood up on his hind legs and talked like a man.

The moon was just going down when Mowgli and the two wolves came to the hill of the Council Rock, and they stopped at Mother Wolf's cave.

"They have cast me out from the Man-Pack, Mother," shouted Mowgli, "but I come with the hide of Shere Khan to keep my word."

Mother Wolf walked stiffly from the cave with

the cubs behind her, and her eyes glowed as she saw the skin.

"I told him on that day, when he crammed his head and shoulders into this cave, hunting for your life, Little Frog – I told him that the hunter would be the hunted. It is well done."

"Little Brother, it is well done," said a deep voice in the thicket. "We were lonely in the jungle without you," and Bagheera came running to Mowgli's bare feet. They clambered up the Council Rock together, and Mowgli spread the skin out on the flat stone where Akela used to sit, and pegged it down with four slivers of bamboo, and Akela lay down upon it, and called the old call to the Council, "Look – look well, O Wolves," exactly as he had called when Mowgli was first brought there.

Ever since Akela had been deposed, the Pack had been without a leader, hunting and fighting at their own pleasure. But they answered the call from habit; and some of them were lame from the traps they had fallen into, and some limped from shot wounds, and some were mangy from eating bad food, and many were missing. But they came to the Council Rock, all that were left of them, and saw Shere Khan's striped hide on the rock, and the huge claws dangling at the end of the empty dangling feet. It was then that Mowgli made up a song that came up into his throat all by itself, and he shouted it aloud, leaping up and down on the rattling skin, and beating time with his heels till he had no more breath left, while Grey Brother and Akela howled between the verses.

"Look well, O Wolves. Have I kept my word?" said Mowgli. And the wolves bayed "Yes," and one tattered wolf howled:

"Lead us again, O Akela. Lead us again, O Man-cub, for we are sick of this lawlessness, and we want to be the Free People once more."

"Nay," purred Bagheera, "that may not be. When ye are full fed, the madness may come upon you again. Not for nothing are ye called the Free People. Ye fought for freedom, and it is yours. Eat it, O Wolves."

"Man-Pack and Wolf-Pack have cast me out," said Mowgli. "Now I will hunt alone in the jungle."

"And we will hunt with you," said the four cubs.

So Mowgli went away and hunted with the four cubs in the jungle from that day on. But he was not always alone, because, years afterward, he became a man and married.

But that is a story for grown-ups.

MOWGLI'S SONG

(THAT HE SANG AT THE COUNCIL ROCK WHEN HE DANCED ON SHERE KHAN'S HIDE)

*The Song of Mowgli – I, Mowgli, am singing. Let the jungle
listen to the things I have done.
Shere Khan said he would kill – would kill! At the gates in the
twilight he would kill Mowgli, the Frog!
He ate and he drank. Drink deep, Shere Khan, for when will
you drink again? Sleep and dream of the kill.
I am alone on the grazing grounds. Grey Brother, come to me!
Come to me, Lone Wolf, for there is big game afoot!
Bring up the great bull buffaloes, the blue-skinned herd bulls
with the angry eyes. Drive them to and fro as I order.
Sleep you still, Shere Khan? Wake, oh, wake! Here come I,
and the bulls are behind.
Rama, the King of the Buffaloes, stamped with his foot.
Waters of the Waingunga, where went Shere Khan?
He is not Ikki to dig holes, nor Mao, the Peacock, that he
should fly. He is not Mang the Bat, to hang in the
branches. Little bamboos that creak together, tell me
where he ran?*

Ow! *He is there.* Ahoo! *He is there. Under the feet of Rama
lies the Lame One! Up, Shere Khan! Up and kill! Here
is meat; break the necks of the bulls!*

Hush! *He is asleep. We will not wake him, for his strength is
very great. The kites have come down to see it. The
black ants have come up to know it. There is a great
assembly in his honour.*

Alala! *I have no cloth to wrap me. The kites will see that I am
naked. I am ashamed to meet all these people.*

*Lend me your coat, Shere Khan. Lend me your striped coat so
that I may go to the Council Rock.*

*By the Bull that bought me I made a promise –
a little promise. Only your coat is lacking before I keep
my word.*

*With the knife, with the knife that men use, with the knife of
the hunter, I will stoop down for my gift.*

*Waters of the Waingunga, Shere Khan gives me his coat for
the love that he bears me. Pull, Grey Brother! Pull,
Akela! Heavy is the hide of Shere Khan.*

*The Man Pack are angry. They throw stones and talk child's
talk. My mouth is bleeding. Let me run away.*

"Tiger! Tiger!"

*Through the night, through the hot night, run swiftly with me,
my brothers. We will leave the lights of the village and
go to the low moon.*

*Waters of the Waingunga, the Man-Pack have cast me out. I
did them no harm, but they were afraid of me. Why?*

*Wolf Pack, ye have cast me out too. The jungle is shut
to me and the village gates are shut. Why?*

*As Mang flies between the beasts and birds, so fly I between
the village and the jungle. Why?*

*I dance on the hide of Shere Khan, but my heart is very
heavy. My mouth is cut and wounded with the stones
from the village, but my heart is very light, because I
have come back to the jungle. Why?*

*These two things fight together in me as the snakes fight in the
spring. The water comes out of my eyes; yet I laugh
while it falls. Why?*

*I am two Mowglis, but the hide of Shere Khan is
under my feet.*

*All the jungle knows that I have killed Shere Khan.
Look, look well, O Wolves!*

*Ahae! My heart is heavy with the things that I do
not understand.*

The White Seal

Oh! hush you, my baby, the night is behind us,
And black are the waters that sparkled so green.
The moon, o'er the combers, looks downward to find us
At rest in the hollows that rustle between.
Where billow meets billow, there soft be your pillow,
Ah, weary wee flipperling, curl at your ease!
The storm shall not wake you, nor shark overtake you,
Asleep in the arms of the slow-swinging seas!

SEAL LULLABY

ALL these things happened several years ago at a place called Novastoshnah, or North East Point, on the Island of St Paul, away and away in the Bering Sea. Limmershin, the Winter Wren, told me the tale when he was blown on to the rigging of a steamer going to Japan, and I took him down into my cabin and warmed and fed him for a couple of days till he was fit to fly back to St Paul's again. Limmershin is a very quaint little bird, but he knows how to tell the truth.

Nobody comes to Novastoshnah except on business, and the only people who have regular business there are the seals. They come in the summer months by hundreds and hundreds of thousands out of the cold grey sea. For Novastoshnah Beach has the finest accommodation for seals of any place in all the world.

Sea Catch knew that, and every spring would swim from whatever place he happened to be in – would swim like a torpedo boat straight for Novastoshnah and spend a month fighting with his companions for a good place on the rocks, as

close to the sea as possible. Sea Catch was fifteen years old, a huge grey fur seal with almost a mane on his shoulders, and long, wicked dog teeth. When he heaved himself up on his front flippers he stood more than four feet clear of the ground, and his weight, if anyone had been bold enough to weigh him, was nearly seven hundred pounds. He was scarred all over with the marks of savage fights, but he was always ready for just one fight more. He would put his head on one side, as though he were afraid to look his enemy in the face; then he would shoot it out like lightning, and when the big teeth were firmly fixed on the other seal's neck, the other seal might get away if he could, but Sea Catch would not help him.

Yet Sea Catch never chased a beaten seal, for that was against the Rules of the Beach. He only wanted room by the sea for his nursery. But as there were forty or fifty thousand other seals hunting for the same thing each spring, the whistling, bellowing, roaring, and blowing on the beach was something frightful.

From a little hill called Hutchinson's Hill, you could look over three and a half miles of ground covered with fighting seals; and the surf was dotted all over with the heads of seals hurrying to land and begin their share of the fighting. They fought in the breakers, they fought in the sand, and they fought on the smooth-worn basalt rocks of the nurseries, for they were just as stupid and unaccommodating as men. Their wives never came to the island until late in May or early in June, for they did not care to be torn to pieces; and the young two-, three-, and four-year-old seals who had not begun housekeeping went inland about half a mile through the ranks of the fighters and played about on the sand dunes in droves and legions, and rubbed off every single green thing that grew. They were called the holluschickie – the bachelors – and there were perhaps two or three hundred thousand of them at Novastoshnah alone.

Sea Catch had just finished his forty-fifth fight one spring when Matkah, his soft, sleek, gentle-eyed wife, came up out of the sea, and he caught her by the scruff of the neck and dumped her down on his reservation, saying gruffly: "Late as usual. Where *have* you been?"

It was not the fashion for Sea Catch to eat anything during the four months he stayed on the beaches, and so his temper was generally bad. Matkah knew better than to answer back. She looked round and cooed: "How thoughtful of you. You've taken the old place again."

"I should think I had," said Sea Catch. "Look at me!"

He was scratched and bleeding in twenty places; one eye was almost out, and his sides were torn to ribbons.

"Oh, you men, you men!" Matkah said, fanning herself with her hind flipper. "Why can't you be sensible and settle your places quietly? You look as though you had been fighting with the killer whale."

"I haven't been doing anything *but* fight since the middle of May. The beach is disgracefully crowded this season. I've met at least a hundred seals from Lukannon Beach, house hunting. Why can't people stay where they belong?"

"I've often thought we should be much happier if we hauled out at Otter Island instead of this crowded place," said Matkah.

"*Bah!* Only the holluschickie go to Otter Island.
If we went there they would say we were afraid."

Sea Catch sunk his head proudly between his
fat shoulders and pretended to go to sleep for a
few minutes, but all the time he was keeping a
sharp lookout for a fight. Now that all the seals
and their wives were on the land, you could hear
their clamour miles out to sea above the loudest
gales. At the lowest counting there were over a
million seals on the beach – old seals, mother
seals, tiny babies, and holluschickie, fighting,
scuffling, bleating, crawling, and playing together
– going down to the sea and coming up from it in
gangs and regiments, lying over every foot of
ground as far as the eye could reach, and
skirmishing about in brigades through the fog. It
is nearly always foggy at Novastoshnah, except
when the sun comes out and makes everything
look all pearly and rainbow-coloured for a little
while.

Kotick, Matkah's baby, was born in the middle
of that confusion, and he was all head and
shoulders, with pale, watery blue eyes, as tiny
seals must be, but there was something about his

coat that made his mother look at him very closely.

"Sea Catch," she said, at last, "our baby's going to be white!"

"Empty clam-shells and dry seaweed!" snorted Sea Catch. "There never has been such a thing in the world as a white seal."

"I can't help that," said Matkah; "there's going to be now." And she sang the low, crooning seal song that all the mother seals sing to their babies:

> You mustn't swim till you're six weeks old,
> Or your head will be sunk by your heels;
> And summer gales and killer whales
> Are bad for baby seals.
>
> Are bad for baby seals, dear rat,
> As bad as bad can be;
> But splash and grow strong,
> And you can't be wrong.
> Child of the Open Sea!

Of course the little fellow did not understand the words at first. He paddled and scrambled about by his mother's side, and learned to scuffle out of the way when his father was fighting with another seal, and the two rolled and roared up and down the slippery rocks. Matkah used to go to sea to get things to eat, and the baby was fed only once in two days, but then he ate all he could and throve upon it.

The first thing he did was to crawl inland, and there he met tens of thousands of babies of his own age, and they played together like puppies, went to sleep on the clean sand, and played again. The old people in the nurseries took no notice of them, and the holluschickie kept to their own grounds, and the babies had a beautiful playtime.

When Matkah came back from her deep-sea fishing she would go straight to their playground and call as a sheep calls for a lamb, and wait until she heard Kotick bleat. Then she would take the straightest of straight lines in his direction, striking out with her fore flippers and knocking the youngsters head over heels right and left. There were always a few hundred mothers hunting for their children through the playgrounds, and the babies were kept lively. But, as Matkah told Kotick, "So long as you don't lie in muddy water and get mange, or rub the hard sand into a cut or scratch, and so long as you never go swimming when there is a heavy sea, nothing will hurt you here."

Little seals can no more swim than little children, but they are unhappy till they learn. The first time that Kotick went down to the sea a wave carried him out beyond his depth, and his big head sank and his little hind flippers flew up exactly as his mother had told him in the song, and if the next wave had not thrown him back again he would have drowned.

After that, he learned to lie in a beach pool and let the wash of the waves just cover him and lift him up while he paddled, but he always kept his eye open for big waves that might hurt. He was two weeks learning to use his flippers; and all that while he floundered in and out of the water, and coughed and grunted and crawled up the beach and took catnaps on the sand, and went back again, until at last he found that he truly belonged to the water.

Then you can imagine the times that he had

with his companions, ducking under the rollers;
or coming in on top of a comber and landing
with a swash and a splutter as the big wave went
whirling far up the beach; or standing up on his
tail and scratching his head as the old people did;
or playing 'I'm the King of the Castle' on slippery,
weedy rocks that just stuck out of the wash. Now
and then he would see a thin fin, like a big shark's
fin, drifting along close to shore, and he knew
that that was the killer whale, also called the
Grampus, who eats young seals when he can get
them; and Kotick would head for the beach like
an arrow, and the fin would jig off slowly, as if it
were looking for nothing at all.

Late in October the seals began to leave
St Paul's for the deep sea, by families and tribes,
and there was no more fighting over the
nurseries, and the holluschickie played anywhere
they liked. "Next year," said Matkah to Kotick,
"you will be a holluschickie; but this year you
must learn how to catch fish."

They set out together across the Pacific, and
Matkah showed Kotick how to sleep on his back
with his flippers tucked down by his side and his

little nose just out of the water. No cradle is so comfortable as the long, rocking swell of the Pacific. When Kotick felt his skin tingle all over, Matkah told him he was learning the 'feel of the water,' and that tingly, prickly feelings meant bad weather coming, and he must swim hard and get away.

"In a little time," she said, "you'll know where to swim to, but just now we'll follow Sea Pig, the Porpoise, for he is very wise." A school of porpoises were ducking and tearing through the water, and little Kotick followed them as fast as he could. "How do you know where to go to?" he panted. The leader of the school rolled his white eye and ducked under. "My tail tingles, youngster," he said. "That means there's a gale behind me. Come along! When you're south of the Sticky Water [he meant the Equator] and your tail tingles, that means there's a gale in front of you and you must head north. Come along! The water feels bad here."

This was one of very many things that Kotick learned, and he was always learning. Matkah taught him to follow the cod and the halibut

along the under-sea banks and wrench the
rockling out of his hole among the weeds; how to
skirt the wrecks lying a hundred fathoms below
water and dart like a rifle bullet in at one
porthole and out at another as the fishes ran;
how to dance on the top of the waves when the
lightning was racing all over the sky, and wave his
flipper politely to the stumpy-tailed Albatross
and the Man-of-war Hawk as they went down
the wind; how to jump three or four feet clear of
the water like a dolphin, flippers close to the side
and tail curved; to leave the flying fish alone
because they are all bony; to take the shoulder-
piece out of a cod at full speed ten fathoms deep,
and never to stop and look at a boat or a ship,
and particularly not a rowing-boat. At the end of
six months what Kotick did not know about
deep-sea fishing was not worth the knowing. And
all that time he never set flipper on dry ground.

One day, however, as he was lying half asleep in
the warm water somewhere off the Island of Juan
Fernandez, he felt faint and lazy all over, just as
human people do when the spring is in their legs,
and he remembered the good firm beaches of

The White Seal

Novastoshnah seven thousand miles away, the games his companions played, the smell of the seaweed, the seal roar, and the fighting. That very minute he turned north, swimming steadily, and as he went on he met scores of his mates, all bound for the same place, and they said: "Greeting, Kotick! This year we are all holluschickie, and we can dance the Fire-dance in the breakers off Lukannon and play on the new grass. But where did you get that coat?"

Kotick's fur was almost pure white now, and though he felt very proud of it, he only said, "Swim quickly! My bones are aching for the land." And so they all came to the beaches where they had been born, and heard the old seals, their fathers, fighting in the rolling mist.

That night Kotick danced the Fire-dance with the yearling seals. The sea is full of fire on summer nights all the way down from Novastoshnah to Lukannon, and each seal leaves a wake like burning oil behind him and a flaming flash when he jumps, and the waves break in great phosphorescent streaks and swirls. Then they went inland to the holluschickie grounds and rolled up and down in the new wild wheat and told stories of what they had done while they had been at sea. They talked about the Pacific as boys would talk about a wood that they had been exploring in, and if anyone had understood them he could have gone away and made such a chart of that ocean as never was. The three- and four-year-old holluschickie romped down from Hutchinson's Hill crying: "Out of the way, youngsters! The sea is deep and you don't know all that's in it yet. Wait till you've rounded the Horn. Hi, you yearling, where did you get that white coat?"

"I didn't get it," said Kotick. "It grew." And just as he was going to roll the speaker over, a couple of black-haired men with flat red faces came from behind a sand dune, and Kotick, who had never seen a man before, coughed and lowered his head. The holluschickie just bundled off a few yards and sat staring stupidly. The men were no less than Kerick Booterin, the chief of the seal hunters on the island, and Patalamon, his son. They came from the little village not half a mile from the sea nurseries, and they were deciding what seals they would drive up to the killing pens – for the seals were driven just like sheep – to be turned into sealskin jackets later on.

"Ho!" said Patalamon. "Look! There's a white seal!"

Kerick Booterin turned nearly white. Then he began to mutter a prayer. "Don't touch him, Patalamon. There has never been a white seal since – since I was born. Perhaps it is old Zaharrof's ghost. He was lost last year in the big gale."

"I'm not going near him," said Patalamon. "He's unlucky. Do you really think he is old Zaharrof come back? I owe him for some gulls' eggs."

"Don't look at him," said Kerick. "Head off that group of four-year-olds. The men ought to skin two hundred today, but it's the beginning of the season and they are new to the work. A hundred will do. Quick!"

Patalamon rattled a pair of seal's shoulder bones in front of a herd of holluschickie and they stopped dead, puffing and blowing. Then he stepped near and the seals began to move, and Kerick headed them inland, and they never tried to get back to their companions. Hundreds and hundreds of thousands of seals watched them being driven, but they went on playing just the same. Kotick was the only one who asked questions, and none of his companions could tell him anything, except that the men always drove seals in that way for six weeks or two months of every year.

"I am going to follow," he said, and his eyes nearly popped out of his head as he shuffled along in the wake of the herd.

"The white seal is coming after us," cried Patalamon. "That's the first time a seal has ever come to the killing grounds alone."

"Hush! Don't look behind you," said Kerick. "It is Zaharrof's ghost! I must speak to the priest about this."

The distance to the killing grounds was only half a mile, but it took an hour to cover, because if the seals went too fast Kerick knew that they would get heated and then their fur would come off in patches when they were skinned. So they went on very slowly, past Sea Lion's Neck, past Webster House, till they came to the Salt House

just beyond the sight of the seals on the beach.
Kotick followed, panting and wondering. He
thought that he was at the world's end, but the
roar of the seal nurseries behind him sounded as
loud as the roar of a train in a tunnel. Then
Kerick sat down on the moss and pulled out a
heavy pewter watch and let the drove cool off for
thirty minutes, and Kotick could hear the fog-
dew dripping off the brim of his cap. Then ten or
twelve men, each with an iron-bound club three
or four feet long, came up, and Kerick pointed
out one or two of the drove that were bitten by
their companions or too hot, and the men kicked
those aside with their heavy boots made of the
skin of a walrus's throat, and then Kerick said,
"Let go!" and then the men clubbed the seals on
the head as fast as they could.

Ten minutes later little Kotick did not
recognize his friends any more, for their skins
were ripped off from the nose to the hind
flippers, whipped off and thrown down on the
ground in a pile. That was enough for Kotick. He
turned and galloped (a seal can gallop very swiftly
for a short time) back to the sea; his little new

moustache bristling with horror. At Sea Lion's Neck, where the great sea lions sit on the edge of the surf, he flung himself flipper-overhead into the cool water and rocked there, gasping miserably. "What's here?" said a sea lion gruffly, for as a rule the sea lions keep themselves to themselves.

"*Scoochnie! Ochen scoochnie!*" ("I'm lonesome, very lonesome!") said Kotick. "They're killing *all* the holluschickie on *all* the beaches!"

The Sea Lion turned his head inshore. "Nonsense!" he said. "Your friends are making as much noise as ever. You must have seen old Kerick polishing off a group. He's done that for thirty years."

"It's horrible," said Kotick, backing water as a wave went over him, and steadying himself with a screw stroke of his flippers that brought him all standing within three inches of a jagged edge of rock.

"Well done for a yearling!" said the Sea Lion, who could appreciate good swimming. "I suppose it is rather awful from your way of looking at it, but if you seals will come here year after year, of course the men get to know of it, and unless you can find an island where no men ever come you will always be hunted."

"Isn't there any such island?" began Kotick.

"I've followed the *poltoos* [the halibut] for twenty years, and I can't say I've found it yet. But look here – you seem to have a fondness for talking to your betters – suppose you go to Walrus Islet and talk to Sea Vitch. He may know something. Don't flounce off like that. It's a six-mile swim, and if I were you I should haul out and take a nap first, little one."

Kotick thought that that was good advice, so he swam round to his own beach, hauled out, and slept for half an hour, twitching all over, as seals will. Then he headed straight for Walrus Islet, a little low sheet of rocky island almost due northeast from Novastoshnah, all ledges and rock and gulls' nests, where the walrus herded by themselves.

He landed close to old Sea Vitch – the big, ugly, bloated, pimpled, fat-necked, long-tusked walrus of the North Pacific, who has no manners except when he is asleep – as he was then, with his hind flippers half in and half out of the surf.

"Wake up!" barked Kotick, for the gulls were making a great noise.

"Hah! Ho! Hmph! What's that?" said Sea Vitch, and he struck the next walrus a blow with his tusks and woke him up, and the next struck the next, and so on till they were all awake and staring in every direction but the right one.

"Hi! It's me," said Kotick, bobbing in the surf and looking like a little white slug.

"Well! May I be – skinned!" said Sea Vitch, and they all looked at Kotick as you can fancy a room full of drowsy old gentlemen would look at a little boy. Kotick did not care to hear any more about skinning just then; he had seen enough of it. So he called out: "Isn't there any place for seals to go where men don't ever come?"

"Go and find out," said Sea Vitch, shutting his eyes. "Run away. We're busy here."

Kotick made his dolphin-jump in the air and shouted as loud as he could: "Clam-eater! Clam-eater!" He knew that Sea Vitch never caught a fish in his life but always rooted for clams and seaweed; though he pretended to be a very terrible person. Naturally the Chickies and the Gooverooskies and the Epatkas – the Burgomaster Gulls and the Kittiwakes and the Puffins, who are always looking for a chance to be rude, took up the cry, and – so Limmershin told me – for nearly five minutes you could not have heard a gun fired on Walrus Islet. All the population was yelling and screaming "Clam-eater! *Stareek* [old man]!" while Sea Vitch rolled from side to side grunting and coughing.

"*Now* will you tell?" said Kotick, all out of breath.

"Go and ask Sea Cow," said Sea Vitch. "If he is living still, he'll be able to tell you."

"How shall I know Sea Cow when I meet him?" said Kotick, sheering off.

"He's the only thing in the sea uglier than Sea Vitch," screamed a Burgomaster gull, wheeling under Sea Vitch's nose. "Uglier, and with worse manners! *Stareek*!"

Kotick swam back to Novastoshnah, leaving the gulls to scream. There he found that no one sympathized with him in his little attempt to discover a quiet place for the seals. They told him that men had always driven the holluschickie – it was part of the day's work – and that if he did not like to see ugly things he should not have gone to the killing grounds. But none of the other seals had seen the killing, and that made the difference between him and his friends. Besides, Kotick was a white seal.

"What you must do," said old Sea Catch, after he had heard his son's adventures, "is to grow up and be a big seal like your father, and have a nursery on the beach, and then they will leave you alone. In another five years you ought to be able to fight for yourself." Even gentle Matkah, his mother, said: "You will never be able to stop the killing. Go and play in the sea, Kotick." And Kotick went off and danced the Fire-dance with a very heavy little heart.

That autumn he left the beach as soon as he could, and set off alone because of a notion in his bullet head. He was going to find Sea Cow, if there was such a person in the sea, and he was going to find a quiet island with good firm beaches for seals to live on, where men could not get at them. So he explored and explored by himself from the North to the South Pacific, swimming as much as three hundred miles in a day and a night. He met with more adventures than can be told, and narrowly escaped being caught by the Basking Shark, and the Spotted Shark, and the Hammerhead, and he met all the untrustworthy ruffians that loaf up and down the seas, and the heavy polite fish, and the scarlet spotted scallops that are moored in one place for hundreds of years, and grow very proud of it; but he never met Sea Cow, and he never found an island that he could fancy.

If the beach was good and hard, with a slope behind it for seals to play on, there was always the smoke of a whaler on the horizon, boiling down blubber, and Kotick knew what that meant. Or else he could see that seals had once visited the island and been killed off, and Kotick knew that where men had come once they would come again.

He picked up with an old stumpy-tailed albatross, who told him that Kerguelen Island was the very place for peace and quiet, and when Kotick went down there he was all but smashed to pieces against some wicked black cliffs in a heavy sleet storm with lightning and thunder. Yet as he pulled out against the gale he could see that even there had once been a seal nursery. And it was so in all the other islands that he visited.

Limmershin gave a long list of them, for he said that Kotick spent five seasons exploring, with a four months' rest each year at Novastoshnah, when the holluschickie used to make fun of him and his imaginary islands. He went to the Galapagos, a horrid dry place on the Equator, where he was nearly baked to death; he went to the Georgia Islands, the Orkneys, Emerald Island, Little Nightingale Island, Gough Island, Bouvet's Island, the Crozets, and even to a little speck of an island south of the Cape of Good Hope. But everywhere the People of the Sea told him the same things. Seals had come to those islands once upon a time, but men had killed them all off. Even when he swam thousands of miles out of the Pacific and got to a place called Cape Corientes (that was when he was coming back from Gough Island), he found a few hundred mangy seals on a rock and they told him that men came there too.

That nearly broke his heart, and he headed round the Horn back to his own beaches; and on his way north he hauled out on an island full of green trees, where he found an old, old seal who was dying, and Kotick caught fish for him and told him all his sorrows. "Now," said Kotick, "I am going back to Novastoshnah, and if I am driven to the killing pens with the holluschickie I shall not care."

The old seal said, "Try once more. I am the last of the Lost Rookery of Más Afuera, and in the days when men killed us by the hundred thousand there was a story on the beaches that some day a white seal would come out of the North and lead the seal people to a quiet place. I am old, and I shall never live to see that day, but others will. Try once more."

And Kotick curled up his moustache (it was a beauty) and said, "I am the only white seal that has ever been born on the beaches, and I am the only seal, black or white, who ever thought of looking for new islands."

This cheered him immensely; and when he

came back to Novastoshnah that summer,
Matkah, his mother, begged him to marry and
settle down, for he was no longer a holluschick
but a full-grown sea-catch, with a curly white
mane on his shoulders, as heavy, as big, and as
fierce as his father. "Give me another season," he
said. "Remember, Mother, it is always the seventh
wave that goes farthest up the beach."

Curiously enough, there was another seal who
thought that she would put off marrying till the
next year, and Kotick danced the Fire-dance with
her all down Lukannon Beach the night before he
set off on his last exploration. This time he went
westward, because he had fallen on the trail of a
great shoal of halibut, and he needed at least one
hundred pounds of fish a day to keep him in
good condition. He chased them till he was tired,
and then he curled himself up and went to sleep
on the hollows of the ground swell that sets in to
Copper Island. He knew the coast perfectly well,
so about midnight, when he felt himself gently
bumped on a weed bed, he said, "*Hm*, tide's
running strong tonight," and turning over under
water opened his eyes slowly and stretched. Then

he jumped like a cat, for he saw huge things
nosing about in the shoal water and browsing on
the heavy fringes of the weeds.

"By the Great Combers of Magellan!" he said,
beneath his moustache. "Who in the Deep Sea
are these people?"

They were like no walrus, sea lion, seal, bear,
whale, shark, fish, squid, or scallop that Kotick
had ever seen before. They were between twenty
and thirty feet long, and they had no hind
flippers, but a shovel-like tail that looked as if it
had been whittled out of wet leather. Their heads
were the most foolish-looking things you ever
saw, and they balanced on the ends of their tails
in deep water when they weren't grazing, bowing
solemnly to each other and waving their front
flippers as a fat man waves his arm.

"*Ahem!*" said Kotick. "Good sport, gentlemen?"
The big things answered by bowing and waving
their flippers like the Frog Footman. When they
began feeding again Kotick saw that their upper
lip was split into two pieces that they could
twitch apart about a foot and bring together
again with a whole bushel of seaweed between

the splits. They tucked the stuff into their mouths and chumped solemnly.

"Messy style of feeding, that," said Kotick. They bowed again, and Kotick began to lose his temper. "Very good," he said. "If you *do* happen to have an extra joint in your front flipper you needn't show off so. I see you bow gracefully, but I should like to know your names." The split lips moved and twitched; and the glassy green eyes stared, but they did not speak.

"Well!" said Kotick. "You're the only people I've ever met uglier than Sea Vitch – and with worse manners."

Then he remembered in a flash what the Burgomaster gull had screamed to him when he was a little yearling at Walrus Islet, and he tumbled backward in the water, for he knew that he had found Sea Cow at last.

The sea cows went on schlooping and grazing and chumping in the weed, and Kotick asked them questions in every language that he had picked up in his travels; and the Sea People talk nearly as many languages as human beings. But the sea cows did not answer because Sea Cow

cannot talk. He has only six bones in his neck
where he ought to have seven, and they say under
the sea that that prevents him from speaking
even to his companions. But, as you know, he has
an extra joint in his foreflipper, and by waving it
up and down and about he makes what answers
to a sort of clumsy code.

By daylight Kotick's mane was standing on end
and his temper was gone where the dead crabs go.
Then the Sea Cow began to travel northward
very slowly, stopping to hold absurd bowing
councils from time to time, and Kotick followed
them, saying to himself, "People who are such
idiots as these are would have been killed long
ago if they hadn't found out some safe island.
And what is good enough for the Sea Cow is
good enough for the Sea Catch. All the same, I
wish they'd hurry."

It was weary work for Kotick. The herd never
went more than forty or fifty miles a day, and
stopped to feed at night, and kept close to the
shore all the time; while Kotick swam round
them, and over them, and under them, but he
could not hurry them up one half mile. As they

went farther north they held a bowing council every few hours, and Kotick nearly bit off his moustache with impatience till he saw that they were following up a warm current of water, and then he respected them more.

One night they sank through the shiny water – sank like stones – and for the first time since he had known them began to swim quickly. Kotick followed, and the pace astonished him, for he never dreamed that Sea Cow was anything of a swimmer. They headed for a cliff by the shore – a cliff that ran down into deep water, and plunged into a dark hole at the foot of it, twenty fathoms under the sea. It was a long, long swim, and Kotick badly wanted fresh air before he was out of the dark tunnel they led him through.

"My word!" he said, when he rose, gasping and puffing, into open water at the farther end. "It was a long dive, but it was worth it."

The sea cows had separated and were browsing lazily along the edges of the finest beaches that Kotick had ever seen. There were long stretches of smooth-worn rock running for miles, exactly fitted to make seal-nurseries, and there were playgrounds of hard sand sloping inland behind them, and there were rollers for seals to dance in, and long grass to roll in, and sand dunes to climb up and down, and, best of all, Kotick knew by the feel of the water, which never deceives a true sea catch, that no men had ever come there.

The first thing he did was to assure himself that the fishing was good, and then he swam along the beaches and counted up the delightful low sandy islands half hidden in the beautiful rolling fog. Away to the northward, out to sea, ran a line of bars and shoals and rocks that would never let a ship come within six miles of the beach, and between the islands and the mainland was a stretch of deep water that ran up to the perpendicular cliffs, and somewhere below the cliffs was the mouth of the tunnel.

"It's Novastoshnah over again, but ten times better," said Kotick. "Sea Cow must be wiser than I thought. Men can't come down the cliffs, even if there were any men; and the shoals to seaward would knock a ship to splinters. If any place in the sea is safe, this is it."

He began to think of the seal he had left behind him, but though he was in a hurry to go back to Novastoshnah, he thoroughly explored the new country, so that he would be able to answer all questions.

Then he dived and made sure of the mouth of the tunnel, and raced through to the southward. No one but a sea cow or a seal would have dreamed of there being such a place, and when he looked back at the cliffs even Kotick could hardly believe that he had been under them.

He was six days going home, though he was not swimming slowly; and when he hauled out just above Sea Lion's Neck the first person he met was the seal who had been waiting for him, and she saw by the look in his eyes that he had found his island at last.

But the holluschickie, his father, and all the other seals laughed when he told them what he had discovered, and a young seal about his own age said, "This is all very well, Kotick, but you can't come from no one knows where and order us off like this. Remember we've been fighting for our nurseries, and that's a thing you never did.

You preferred prowling about in the sea."

The other seals laughed at this, and the young seal began twisting his head from side to side. He had just married that year, and was making a great fuss about it.

"I've no nursery to fight for," said Kotick. "I only want to show you all a place where you will be safe. What's the use of fighting?"

"Oh, if you're trying to back out, of course I've no more to say," said the young seal with an ugly chuckle.

"Will you come with me if I win?" said Kotick. And a green light came into his eye, for he was very angry at having to fight at all.

"Very good," said the young seal carelessly. "If you win, I'll come."

He had no time to change his mind, for Kotick's head was out and his teeth sunk in the blubber of the young seal's neck. Then he threw himself back on his haunches and hauled his enemy down the beach, shook him, and knocked him over.

Then Kotick roared to the seals: "I've done my best for you these five seasons past. I've found you the island where you'll be safe, but unless your heads are dragged off your silly necks you won't believe. I'm going to teach you now. Look out for yourselves!"

Limmershin told me that never in his life – and Limmershin sees ten thousand big seals fighting every year – never in all his little life did he see anything like Kotick's charge into the nurseries. He flung himself at the biggest sea catch he could find, caught him by the throat, choked him and bumped him and banged him till he grunted for mercy, and then threw him aside and attacked the next.

You see, Kotick had never fasted for four months as the big seals did every year, and his deep-sea swimming trips kept him in perfect condition, and, best of all, he had never fought before. His curly white mane stood up with rage, and his eyes flamed, and his big dog teeth glistened, and he was splendid to look at. Old Sea Catch, his father, saw him tearing past, hauling the grizzled old seals about as though they had been halibut, and upsetting the young bachelors in all directions; and Sea Catch gave a roar and shouted: "He may be a fool, but he is the best fighter on the beaches! Don't tackle your father, my son! He's with you!"

Kotick roared in answer, and old Sea Catch waddled in with his moustache on end, blowing like a locomotive, while Matkah and the seal that was going to marry Kotick cowered down and admired their menfolk. It was a gorgeous fight, for the two fought as long as there was a seal that dared lift up his head, and when there were none they paraded grandly up and down the beach side by side, bellowing.

At night, just as the Northern Lights were winking and flashing through the fog, Kotick climbed a bare rock and looked down on the scattered nurseries and the torn and bleeding seals. "Now," he said, "I've taught you your lesson."

"My word!" said old Sea Catch, boosting himself up stiffly, for he was fearfully mauled. "The killer whale himself could not have cut them up worse. Son, I'm proud of you, and what's more, I'll come with you to your island."

"Hear you, fat pigs of the sea. Who comes with me to the Sea Cow's tunnel? Answer, or I shall teach you again," roared Kotick.

There was a murmur like the ripple of the tide all up and down the beaches. "We will come," said thousands of tired voices. "We will follow Kotick, the White Seal."

Then Kotick dropped his head between his shoulders and shut his eyes proudly. He was not a white seal any more, but red from head to tail. All the same he would have scorned to look at or touch one of his wounds. A week later he and his army (nearly ten thousand holluschickie and old seals) went away north to the Sea Cow's tunnel, Kotick leading them, and the seals that stayed at Novastoshnah called them idiots.

But next spring, when they all met off the fishing banks of the Pacific, Kotick's seals told such tales of the new beaches beyond Sea Cow's tunnel that more and more seals left Novastoshnah.

Of course it was not all done at once, for the seals are not very clever, and they need a long time to turn things over in their minds, but year after year more seals went away from Novastoshnah, and Lukannon, and the other

nurseries, to the quiet, sheltered beaches where
Kotick sits all the summer through, getting bigger
and fatter and stronger each year, while the
holluschickie play.

LUKANNON

This is the great deep-sea song that all the
St Paul seals sing when they are heading back to
their beaches in the summer. It is a sort of very
sad seal National Anthem.

I met my mates in the morning (and, oh, but I am old!)
Where roaring on the ledges the summer groundswell rolled;
I heard them lift the chorus that drowned the breakers' song –
The Beaches of Lukannon – two million voices strong.

The song of pleasant stations beside the salt lagoons,
The song of blowing squadrons that shuffled
down the dunes,
The song of midnight dances that churned
the sea to flame –
The Beaches of Lukannon – before the sealers came!

I met my mates in the morning (I'll never meet them more!);
They came and went in legions that darkened all the shore.
And o'er the foam-flecked offing as far as voice could reach
We hailed the landing parties and we sang them up the beach.

The White Seal

The Beaches of Lukannon – the winter wheat so tall,
The dripping, crinkled lichens, and the sea-fog
drenching all!
The platforms of our play-ground, all shining
smooth and worn!
The Beaches of Lukannon – the home where we
were born!

I met my mates in the morning, a broken, scattered band.
Men shoot us in the water and club us on the land;
Men drive us to the Salt House like silly sheep and tame,
And still we sing Lukannon–before the sealers came.

Wheel down, wheel down to southward;
oh, Gooverooska, go!
And tell the Deep-Sea Viceroys the story of our woe;
Ere, empty as the shark's egg the tempest
flings ashore,
The Beaches of Lukannon shall know their sons
no more!

"Rikki-Tikki-Tavi"

At the hole where he went in
Red-Eye called to Wrinkle-Skin.
Hear what little Red-Eye saith:
"Nag, come up and dance with death!"
Eye to eye and head to head,
(Keep the measure, Nag).
This shall end when one is dead;
(At your pleasure, Nag).
Turn for turn and twist for twist –
(Run and hide you, Nag).
Hah! The hooded Death has missed!
(Woe betide you, Nag!)

THIS is the story of the great war that Rikki-tikki-tavi fought single-handed, through the bathrooms of the big bungalow in Segowlee cantonment. Darzee, the Tailorbird, helped him, and Chuchundra, the muskrat, who never comes out into the middle of the floor, but always creeps round by the wall, gave him advice, but Rikki-tikki did the real fighting.

He was a mongoose, rather like a little cat in his fur and his tail, but quite like a weasel in his head and his habits. His eyes and the end of his restless nose were pink. He could scratch himself anywhere he pleased with any leg, front or back, that he chose to use. He could fluff up his tail till it looked like a bottle brush, and his war cry as he scuttled through the long grass was: "*Rikk-tikk-tikki-tikki-tchk!*"

One day, a high summer flood washed him out of the burrow where he lived with his father and mother, and carried him, kicking and clucking, down a roadside ditch. He found a little wisp of grass floating there, and clung to it till he lost his senses. When he revived, he was lying in the hot sun on the middle of a garden path, very draggled indeed, and a small boy was saying, "Here's a dead mongoose. Let's have a funeral."

"No," said his mother, "let's take him in and dry him. Perhaps he isn't really dead."

They took him into the house, and a big man picked him up between his finger and thumb and said he was not dead but half choked. So they wrapped him in cotton wool, and warmed him over a little fire, and he opened his eyes and sneezed.

"Now," said the big man (he was an Englishman who had just moved into the bungalow), "don't frighten him, and we'll see what he'll do."

It is the hardest thing in the world to frighten a mongoose, because he is eaten up from nose to tail with curiosity. The motto of all the mongoose family is 'Run and find out,' and Rikki-tikki was a true mongoose. He looked at the cotton wool, decided that it was not good to eat, ran all round the table, sat up and put his fur in order, scratched himself, and jumped on the small boy's shoulder.

"Don't be frightened, Teddy," said his father. "That's his way of making friends."

"Ouch! He's tickling under my chin," said Teddy.

Rikki-tikki looked down between the boy's collar and neck, snuffed at his ear, and climbed down to the floor, where he sat rubbing his nose.

"Good gracious," said Teddy's mother, "and that's a wild creature! I suppose he's so tame because we've been kind to him."

"All mongooses are like that," said her husband. "If Teddy doesn't pick him up by the tail, or try to put him in a cage, he'll run in and out of the house all day long. Let's give him something to eat."

They gave him a little piece of raw meat. Rikki-tikki liked it immensely, and when it was finished he went out into the veranda and sat in the sunshine and fluffed up his fur to make it dry to the roots. Then he felt better.

"There are more things to find out about in this house," he said to himself, "than all my family could find out in all their lives. I shall certainly stay and find out."

He spent all that day roaming over the house. He nearly drowned himself in the bathtubs, put

his nose into the ink on a writing table, and
burned it on the end of the big man's cigar, for he
climbed up in the big man's lap to see how
writing was done. At nightfall he ran into Teddy's
nursery to watch how kerosene lamps were
lighted, and when Teddy went to bed Rikki-tikki
climbed up too. But he was a restless companion,
because he had to get up and attend to every
noise all through the night, and find out what
made it. Teddy's mother and father came in, the
last thing, to look at their boy, and Rikki-tikki
was awake on the pillow. "I don't like that," said
Teddy's mother. "He may bite the child." "He'll do
no such thing," said the father. "Teddy's safer
with that little beast than if he had a bloodhound
to watch him. If a snake came into the nursery
now —"

But Teddy's mother wouldn't think of anything
so awful.

Early in the morning Rikki-tikki came to early
breakfast in the veranda riding on Teddy's
shoulder, and they gave him banana and some
boiled egg. He sat on all their laps one after the
other, because every well-brought-up mongoose

always hopes to be a house mongoose some day and have rooms to run about in; and Rikki-tikki's mother (she used to live in the general's house at Segowlee) had carefully told Rikki what to do if ever he came across white men.

Then Rikki-tikki went out into the garden to see what was to be seen. It was a large garden, only half cultivated, with bushes of roses, lime and orange trees, clumps of bamboos, and thickets of high grass. Rikki-tikki licked his lips. "This is a splendid hunting-ground," he said, and his tail grew bottle-brushy at the thought of it, and he scuttled up and down the garden, snuffing here and there till he heard very sorrowful voices in a thornbush.

It was Darzee, the Tailorbird, and his wife. They had made a beautiful nest by pulling two big leaves together and stitching them up the edges with fibres, and had filled the hollow with cotton and downy fluff. The nest swayed to and fro, as they sat on the rim and cried.

"What is the matter?" asked Rikki-tikki.

"We are very miserable," said Darzee. "One of our babies fell out of the nest yesterday and Nag

ate him."

"*Hm!*" said Rikki-tikki, "that is very sad – but I am a stranger here. Who is Nag?"

Darzee and his wife only cowered down in the nest without answering, for from the thick grass at the foot of the bush there came a low hiss – a horrid cold sound that made Rikki-tikki jump back two clear feet. Then inch by inch out of the grass rose up the head and spread hood of Nag, the big black cobra, and he was five feet long from tongue to tail. When he had lifted one-third of himself clear of the ground, he stayed balancing to and fro exactly as a dandelion balances in the wind, and he looked at Rikki-tikki with the wicked snake's eyes that never change their expression, whatever the snake may be thinking of.

"Who is Nag?" said he. "I am Nag. The great God Brahma put his mark upon all our people, when the first cobra spread his hood to keep the sun off Brahma as he slept. Look, and be afraid!"

He spread out his hood more than ever, and Rikki-tikki saw the spectacle-mark on the back of it that looks exactly like the eye part of a hook-

and-eye fastening. He was afraid for the minute, but it is impossible for a mongoose to stay frightened for any length of time, and though Rikki-tikki had never met a live cobra before, his mother had fed him on dead ones, and he knew that all a grown mongoose's business in life was to fight and eat snakes. Nag knew that too and, at the bottom of his cold heart, he was afraid.

"Well," said Rikki-tikki, and his tail began to fluff up again, "marks or no marks, do you think it is right for you to eat fledglings out of a nest?"

Nag was thinking to himself, and watching the least little movement in the grass behind Rikki-tikki. He knew that mongooses in the garden meant death sooner or later for him and his family, but he wanted to get Rikki-tikki off his guard. So he dropped his head a little, and put it on one side.

"Let us talk," he said. "You eat eggs. Why should not I eat birds?"

"Behind you! Look behind you!" sang Darzee.

Rikki-tikki knew better than to waste time in staring. He jumped up in the air as high as he could go, and just under him whizzed by the head of Nagaina, Nag's wicked wife. She had crept up behind him as he was talking, to make an end of him. He heard her savage hiss as the stroke missed. He came down almost across her back, and if he had been an old mongoose he would have known that then was the time to break her back with one bite; but he was afraid of the terrible lashing return stroke of the cobra. He bit, indeed, but did not bite long enough, and he jumped clear of the whisking tail, leaving Nagaina torn and angry.

"Wicked, wicked Darzee!" said Nag, lashing up as high as he could reach toward the nest in the thornbush. But Darzee had built it out of reach of snakes, and it only swayed to and fro.

Rikki-tikki felt his eyes growing red and hot (when a mongoose's eyes grow red, he is angry), and he sat back on his tail and hind legs like a little kangaroo, and looked all round him, and chattered with rage. But Nag and Nagaina had disappeared into the grass. When a snake misses its stroke, it never says anything or gives any sign of what it means to do next. Rikki-tikki did not care to follow them, for he did not feel sure that he could manage two snakes at once. So he trotted off to the gravel path near the house, and sat down to think. It was a serious matter for him.

If you read the old books of natural history, you will find they say that when the mongoose fights the snake and happens to get bitten, he runs off and eats some herb that cures him. That is not true. The victory is only a matter of quickness of eye and quickness of foot – snake's blow against mongoose's jump – and as no eye can follow the motion of a snake's head when it strikes, this makes things much more wonderful than any magic herb. Rikki-tikki knew he was a young mongoose, and it made him all the more pleased to think that he had managed to escape a blow from behind. It gave him confidence in himself, and when Teddy came running down the path, Rikki-tikki was ready to be petted.

But just as Teddy was stooping, something wriggled a little in the dust, and a tiny voice said: "Be careful. I am Death!" It was Karait, the dusty brown snakeling that lies for choice on the dusty earth; and his bite is as dangerous as the cobra's.

But he is so small that nobody thinks of him, and so he does the more harm to people.

Rikki-tikki's eyes grew red again, and he danced up to Karait with the peculiar rocking, swaying motion that he had inherited from his family. It looks very funny, but it is so perfectly balanced that you can fly off from it at any angle you please, and in dealing with snakes this is an advantage. If Rikki-tikki had only known, he was doing a much more dangerous thing than fighting Nag, for Karait is so small, and can turn so quickly, that unless Rikki bit him close to the back of the head, he would get the return stroke in his eye or his lip. But Rikki did not know. His eyes were all red, and he rocked back and forth, looking for a good place to hold. Karait struck out. Rikki jumped sideways and tried to run in, but the wicked little dusty grey head lashed within a fraction of his shoulder, and he had to jump over the body, and the head followed his heels close.

Teddy shouted to the house: "Oh, look here! Our mongoose is killing a snake." And Rikki-tikki heard a scream from Teddy's mother. His father ran out with a stick, but by the time he came up, Karait had lunged out once too far, and Rikki-tikki had sprung, jumped on the snake's back, dropped his head far between his forelegs, bitten as high up the back as he could get hold, and rolled away. That bite paralyzed Karait, and Rikki-tikki was just going to eat him up from the tail, as is the custom of his family at dinner, when he remembered that a full meal makes a slow mongoose, and if he wanted all his strength and quickness ready, he must keep himself thin.

He went away for a dust bath under the castor-oil bushes, while Teddy's father beat the dead Karait. "What is the use of that?" thought Rikki-tikki. "I have settled it all;" and then Teddy's mother picked him up from the dust and hugged him, crying that he had saved Teddy from death, and Teddy's father said that he was a blessing, and Teddy looked on with big scared eyes. Rikki-tikki was rather amused at all the fuss, which, of course, he did not understand. Teddy's mother might just as well have petted Teddy for playing in the dust. Rikki was thoroughly enjoying himself.

That night at dinner, walking to and fro among the wine glasses on the table, he might have stuffed himself three times over with nice things. But he remembered Nag and Nagaina, and though it was very pleasant to be patted and petted by Teddy's mother, and to sit on Teddy's shoulder, his eyes would get red from time to time, and he would go off into his long war cry of "*Rikk-tikk-tikki-tikki-tchk!*"

Teddy carried him off to bed, and insisted on Rikki-tikki sleeping under his chin. Rikki-tikki was too well bred to bite or scratch, but as soon as Teddy was asleep he went off for his nightly walk round the house, and in the dark he ran up against Chuchundra, the muskrat, creeping around by the wall. Chuchundra is a broken-hearted little beast. He whimpers and cheeps all the night, trying to make up his mind to run into the middle of the room. But he never gets there.

"Don't kill me," said Chuchundra, almost weeping. "Rikki-tikki, don't kill me!"

"Do you think a snake-killer kills muskrats?" said Rikki-tikki scornfully.

"Those who kill snakes get killed by snakes,"

said Chuchundra, more sorrowfully than ever. "And how am I to be sure that Nag won't mistake me for you some dark night?"

"There's not the least danger," said Rikki-tikki. "But Nag is in the garden, and I know you don't go there."

"My cousin Chua, the rat, told me –" said Chuchundra, and then he stopped.

"Told you what?"

"*Hush!* Nag is everywhere, Rikki-tikki. You should have talked to Chua in the garden."

"I didn't – so you must tell me. Quick, Chuchundra, or I'll bite you!"

Chuchundra sat down and cried till the tears rolled off his whiskers. "I am a very poor man," he sobbed. "I never had spirit enough to run out into the middle of the room. *Hush!* I mustn't tell you anything. Can't you *hear*, Rikki-tikki?"

Rikki-tikki listened. The house was as still as still, but he thought he could just catch the faintest *scratch-scratch* in the world – a noise as faint as that of a wasp walking on a windowpane – the dry scratch of a snake's scales on brickwork.

"That's Nag or Nagaina," he said to himself,

"and he is crawling into the bathroom sluice. You're right, Chuchundra; I should have talked to Chua."

He stole off to Teddy's bathroom, but there was nothing there, and then to Teddy's mother's bathroom. At the bottom of the smooth plaster wall there was a brick pulled out to make a sluice for the bath water, and as Rikki-tikki stole in by the masonry curb where the bath is put, he heard Nag and Nagaina whispering together outside in the moonlight.

"When the house is emptied of people," said Nagaina to her husband, "*he* will have to go away, and then the garden will be our own again. Go in quietly, and remember that the big man who killed Karait is the first one to bite. Then come out and tell me, and we will hunt for Rikki-tikki together."

"But are you sure that there is anything to be gained by killing the people?" said Nag.

"Everything. When there were no people in the bungalow, did we have any mongoose in the garden? So long as the bungalow is empty, we are king and queen of the garden; and remember that

as soon as our eggs in the melon bed hatch (as they may tomorrow), our children will need room and quiet."

"I had not thought of that," said Nag. "I will go, but there is no need that we should hunt for Rikki-tikki afterward. I will kill the big man and his wife, and the child if I can, and come away quietly. Then the bungalow will be empty, and Rikki-tikki will go."

Rikki-tikki tingled all over with rage and hatred at this, and then Nag's head came through the sluice, and his five feet of cold body followed it. Angry as he was, Rikki-tikki was very frightened as he saw the size of the big cobra. Nag coiled himself up, raised his head, and looked into the bathroom in the dark, and Rikki could see his eyes glitter.

"Now, if I kill him here, Nagaina will know; and if I fight him on the open floor, the odds are in his favour. What am I to do?" said Rikki-tikki.

Nag waved to and fro, and then Rikki-tikki heard him drinking from the biggest water jar that was used to fill the bath. "That is good," said the snake. "Now, when Karait was killed, the big man had a stick. He may have that stick still, but when he comes in to bathe in the morning he will not have a stick. I shall wait here till he comes. Nagaina – do you hear me? – I shall wait here in the cool till daytime."

There was no answer from outside, so Rikki-tikki knew Nagaina had gone away. Nag coiled himself down, coil by coil, round the bulge at the bottom of the water jar, and Rikki-tikki stayed still. After an hour he began to move, muscle by muscle, toward the jar. Nag was asleep, and Rikki-tikki looked at his big back, wondering which would be the best place for a good hold. "If I don't break his back at the first jump," said Rikki, "he can still fight. And if he fights – O Rikki!" He looked at the thickness of the neck below the hood, but that was too much for him; and a bite near the tail would only make Nag savage.

"It must be the head," he said at last; "the head above the hood. And, when I am once there, I must not let go."

Then he jumped. The head was lying a little clear of the water jar, under the curve of it; and, as his teeth met, Rikki braced his back against the bulge of the red earthenware to hold down the head. This gave him just one second's purchase, and he made the most of it. Then he was battered to and fro as a rat is shaken by a dog – to and fro on the floor, up and down, and around in great circles, but his eyes were red and he held on as the body whipped over the floor, upsetting the tin dipper and the soap dish and the flesh brush, and banged against the tin side of the bath. As he held he closed his jaws tighter and tighter, for he was sure he would be banged to death, and, for the honour of his family, he preferred to be found with his teeth locked. He was dizzy, aching, and felt shaken to pieces when something went off like a thunderclap just behind him. A hot wind knocked him senseless and red fire singed his fur. The big man had been wakened by the noise, and had fired both barrels of a shotgun into Nag just behind the hood.

Rikki-tikki held on with his eyes shut, for now he was quite sure he was dead. But the head did not move, and the big man picked him up and said, "It's the mongoose again, Alice. The little chap has saved *our* lives now."

Then Teddy's mother came in with a very white face, and saw what was left of Nag, and Rikki-tikki dragged himself to Teddy's bedroom and spent half the rest of the night shaking himself tenderly to find out whether he really was broken into forty pieces, as he fancied.

When morning came he was very stiff, but well pleased with his doings. "Now I have Nagaina to settle with, and she will be worse than five Nags, and there's no knowing when the eggs she spoke of will hatch. Goodness! I must go and see Darzee," he said. Without waiting for breakfast, Rikki-tikki ran to the thornbush where Darzee was singing a song of triumph at the top of his voice. The news of Nag's death was all over the garden, for the sweeper had thrown the body on the rubbish-heap.

"Oh, you stupid tuft of feathers!" said Rikki-tikki angrily. "Is this the time to sing?"

"Nag is dead – is dead – is dead!" sang Darzee. "The valiant Rikki-tikki caught him by the head and held fast. The big man brought the bang-stick, and Nag fell in two pieces! He will never eat my babies again."

"All that's true enough. But where's Nagaina?" said Rikki-tikki, looking carefully round him.

"Nagaina came to the bathroom sluice and called for Nag," Darzee went on, "and Nag came out on the end of a stick – the sweeper picked him up on the end of a stick and threw him upon the rubbish heap. Let us sing about the great, the red-eyed Rikki-tikki!" And Darzee filled his throat and sang.

"If I could get up to your nest, I'd roll your babies out!" said Rikki-tikki. "You don't know when to do the right thing at the right time. You're safe enough in your nest there, but it's war for me down here. Stop singing, Darzee."

"For the great, the beautiful Rikki-tikki's sake I will stop," said Darzee. "What is it, O Killer of the terrible Nag?"

"Where is Nagaina, for the third time?"

"On the rubbish heap by the stables, mourning Nag. Great is Rikki-tikki with the white teeth."

"Bother my white teeth! Have you ever heard where she keeps her eggs?"

"In the melon bed, on the end nearest the wall,

where the sun strikes nearly all day. She hid them there weeks ago."

"And you never thought it worthwhile to tell me? The end nearest the wall, you said?"

"Rikki-tikki, you are not going to eat her eggs?"

"Not eat exactly; no. Darzee, if you have a grain of sense you will fly off to the stables and pretend that your wing is broken, and let Nagaina chase you away to this bush. I must get to the melon bed, and if I went there now she'd see me."

Darzee was a feather-brained little fellow who could never hold more than one idea at a time in his head. And just because he knew that Nagaina's children were born in eggs like his own, he didn't think at first that it was fair to kill them. But his wife was a sensible bird, and she knew that cobra's eggs meant young cobras later on. So she flew off from the nest, and left Darzee to keep the babies warm, and continue his song about the death of Nag. Darzee was very like a man in some ways.

She fluttered in front of Nagaina by the rubbish heap and cried out, "Oh, my wing is broken! The boy in the house threw a stone at me and broke it." Then she fluttered more desperately than ever.

Nagaina lifted up her head and hissed, "You warned Rikki-tikki when I would have killed him. Indeed and truly, you've chosen a bad place to be lame in." And she moved toward Darzee's wife, slipping along over the dust.

"The boy broke it with a stone!" shrieked Darzee's wife.

"Well! It may be some consolation to you when you're dead to know that I shall settle accounts with the boy. My husband lies on the rubbish heap this morning, but before night the boy in the house will lie very still. What is the use of running away? I am sure to catch you. Little fool, look at me!"

Darzee's wife knew better than to do *that*, for a bird who looks at a snake's eyes gets so frightened that she cannot move. Darzee's wife fluttered on, piping sorrowfully, and never leaving the ground, and Nagaina quickened her pace.

Rikki-tikki heard them going up the path from the stables, and he raced for the end of the melon

patch near the wall. There, in the warm litter
above the melons, very cunningly hidden, he
found twenty-five eggs, about the size of a hen's
eggs, but with whitish skin instead of shell.

"I was not a day too soon," he said, for he could
see the baby cobras curled up inside the skin, and
he knew that the minute they were hatched they
could each kill a man or a mongoose. He bit off
the tops of the eggs as fast as he could, taking
care to crush the young cobras, and turned over
the litter from time to time to see whether he
had missed any. At last there were only three eggs
left, and Rikki-tikki began to chuckle to himself,
when he heard Darzee's wife screaming:

"Rikki-tikki, I led Nagaina toward the house,
and she has gone into the veranda, and – oh,
come quickly – she means killing!"

Rikki-tikki smashed two eggs, and tumbled
backward down the melon bed with the third
egg in his mouth, and scuttled away as hard as he
could put foot to the ground. Teddy and his
mother and father were there at early breakfast,
but Rikki-tikki saw that they were not eating
anything. They sat stone-still, and their faces were

white. Nagaina was coiled up on the matting by Teddy's chair, within easy striking distance of Teddy's bare leg, and she was swaying to and fro, singing a song of triumph.

"Son of the big man that killed Nag," she hissed, "stay still. I am not ready yet. Wait a little. Keep very still, all you three! If you move I strike, and if you do not move I strike. Oh, foolish people, who killed my Nag!"

Teddy's eyes were fixed on his father, and all his father could do was to whisper, "Sit still, Teddy. You mustn't move. Teddy, keep still."

Then Rikki-tikki came up and cried, "Turn round, Nagaina. Turn and fight!"

"All in good time," said she, without moving her eyes. "I will settle my account with you presently. Look at your friends, Rikki-tikki. They are still and white. They are afraid. They dare not move, and if you come a step nearer I strike."

"Look at your eggs," said Rikki-tikki, "in the melon bed near the wall. Go and look, Nagaina!"

The big snake turned half around, and saw the egg. "Ah-h! Give it to me," she said.

Rikki-tikki put his paws one on each side of

the egg, and his eyes were blood-red. "What price for a snake's egg? For a young cobra? For a young king cobra? For the last – the very last of the brood? The ants are eating all the others down by the melon bed."

Nagaina spun clear round, forgetting everything for the sake of the one egg. Rikki-tikki saw Teddy's father shoot out a big hand, catch Teddy by the shoulder, and drag him across the little table with the tea cups, safe and out of reach of Nagaina.

"Tricked! Tricked! Tricked! *Rikk-tck-tck!*" chuckled Rikki-tikki. "The boy is safe, and it was I – I – I that caught Nag by the hood last night in the bathroom." Then he began to jump up and down, all four feet together, his head close to the floor. "He threw me to and fro, but he could not shake me off. He was dead before the big man blew him in two. I did it! *Rikki-tikki-tck-tck!* Come then, Nagaina. Come and fight with me. You shall not be a widow long."

Nagaina saw that she had lost her chance of killing Teddy, and the egg lay between Rikki-tikki's paws. "Give me the egg, Rikki-tikki. Give me the last of my eggs, and I will go away and never come back," she said, lowering her hood.

"Yes, you will go away, and you will never come back. For you will go to the rubbish heap with Nag. The big man has gone for his gun! Fight!"

Rikki-tikki was bounding all round Nagaina, keeping just out of reach of her stroke, his little eyes like hot coals. Nagaina gathered herself together and flung out at him. Rikki-tikki jumped up and backward. Again and again and again she struck, and each time she gathered herself together like a watch spring. Then Rikki-tikki danced in a circle to get behind her, and Nagaina spun round to keep her head to his head, so that the rustle of her tail sounded like dry leaves blown along by the wind.

He had forgotten the egg. It still lay nearby and Nagaina came nearer and nearer to it, till at last, while Rikki-tikki was drawing breath, she caught it in her mouth and flew like an arrow down the path, with Rikki-tikki behind her. When the cobra runs for her life, she goes like a whiplash flicked across a horse's neck.

Rikki-tikki knew that he must catch her, or all the trouble would begin again. She headed straight for the long grass by the thornbush, and as he was running Rikki-tikki heard Darzee still singing his foolish little song of triumph. But Darzee's wife was wiser. She flew off her nest as Nagaina came along, and flapped her wings about Nagaina's head. If Darzee had helped they might have turned her, but Nagaina only lowered her hood and went on. Still, the instant's delay brought Rikki-tikki up to her, and as she plunged into the rat-hole where she and Nag used to live, his little white teeth were clenched on her tail, and he went down with her – and very few mongooses, however wise and old they may be, care to follow a cobra into its hole. It was dark in the hole; and Rikki-tikki never knew when it might open out and give Nagaina room to turn and strike at him. He held on savagely, and stuck out his feet to act as brakes on the dark slope of the hot, moist earth.

Then the grass by the mouth of the hole stopped waving, and Darzee said, "It is all over with Rikki-tikki! We must sing his death song.

Valiant Rikki-tikki is dead! For Nagaina will
surely kill him underground."

So he sang a very mournful song that he made
up on the spur of the minute, and just as he got
to the most touching part, the grass quivered
again, and Rikki-tikki, covered with dirt, dragged
himself out of the hole leg by leg, licking his
whiskers. Darzee stopped with a little shout.
Rikki-tikki shook some of the dust out of his fur
and sneezed. "It is all over," he said. "The widow
will never come out again." And the red ants that
live between the grass stems heard him, and
began to troop down one after another to see if
he had spoken the truth.

Rikki-tikki curled himself up in the grass and
slept where he was – slept till it was late in the
afternoon, for he had done a hard day's work.

"Now," he said, when he awoke, "I will go back
to the house. Tell the Coppersmith, Darzee, and
he will tell the garden that Nagaina is dead."

The Coppersmith is a bird who makes a noise
exactly like the beating of a little hammer on a
copper pot; and the reason he is always making it
is because he is the town crier to every Indian

garden, and tells all the news to everybody who cares to listen. As Rikki-tikki went up the path, he heard his 'attention' notes like a tiny dinner gong, and then the steady '*Ding-dong-tock!* Nag is dead – *dong!* Nagaina is dead! *Ding-dong-tock!*' That set all the birds in the garden singing, and the frogs croaking, for Nag and Nagaina used to eat frogs as well as little birds.

When Rikki got to the house, Teddy and Teddy's mother (she looked very white still, for she had fainted) and Teddy's father came out and almost cried over him; and that night he ate all that was given him till he could eat no more, and went to bed on Teddy's shoulder, where Teddy's mother saw him when she came to look late at night.

"He saved our lives and Teddy's life," she said to her husband. "Just think, he saved all our lives."

Rikki-tikki woke up with a jump, for the mongooses are light sleepers.

"Oh, it's you," said he. "What are you bothering for? All the cobras are dead. And if they weren't, I'm here."

Rikki-tikki had a right to be proud of himself.

But he did not grow too proud, and he kept that garden as a mongoose should keep it, with tooth and jump and spring and bite, till never a cobra dared show its head inside the walls.

DARZEE'S CHANT
(SUNG IN HONOUR OF RIKKI-TIKKI-TAVI)

Singer and tailor am I –
Doubled the joys that I know –
Proud of my lilt to the sky,
Proud of the house that I sew –
Over and under, so weave I my music – so weave I the house
that I sew.

Sing to your fledglings again,
Mother, oh lift up your head!
Evil that plagued us is slain,
Death in the garden lies dead.
Terror that hid in the roses is impotent – flung on
the dunghill and dead!

Who has delivered us, who?
Tell me his nest and his name.
Rikki, the valiant, the true,
Tikki, with eyeballs of flame,
Rikk-tikki-tikki, the ivory-fanged,
the hunter with eyeballs of flame!

Give him the Thanks of the Birds,
Bowing with tail feathers spread!
Praise him with nightingale words –
Nay, I will praise him instead.
Hear! I will sing you the praise of the bottle-tailed Rikki, with
eyeballs of red!

(Here Rikki-tikki interrupted, and the rest of the song is lost.)

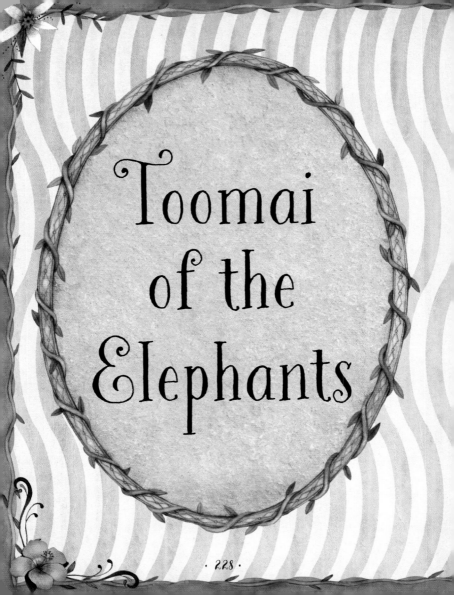

Toomai of the Elephants

I will remember what I was, I am sick of rope and chain –
I will remember my old strength and all my forest affairs.
I will not sell my back to man for a bundle of sugarcane:
I will go out to my own kind, and the wood-folk in their lairs.

I will go out until the day, until the morning break –
Out to the wind's untainted kiss, the water's clean caress;
I will forget my ankle-ring and snap my picket stake.
I will revisit my lost loves, and playmates masterless!

KALA Nag, which means Black Snake, had served the Indian Government in every way that an elephant could serve it for forty-seven years, and as he was fully twenty years old when he was caught, that makes him nearly seventy – a ripe age for an elephant. He remembered pushing, with a big leather pad on his forehead, at a gun stuck in deep mud, and that was before the Afghan War of 1842, and he had not then come to his full strength.

His mother Radha Pyari, – Radha the darling – who had been caught in the same drive with Kala Nag, told him, before his little milk tusks had dropped out, that elephants who were afraid always got hurt. Kala Nag knew that that advice was good, for the first time that he saw a shell burst he backed, screaming, into a stand of piled rifles, and the bayonets pricked him in all his softest places. So, before he was twenty-five, he gave up being afraid, and so he was the best-loved and the best-looked-after elephant in the service of the Government of India. He had carried tents, twelve hundred pounds' weight of tents, on the march in Upper India. He had been hoisted into a ship at the end of a steam crane and taken for days across the water, and made to carry a mortar on his back in a strange and rocky country very far from India, and had seen the Emperor Theodore lying dead in Magdala, and had come back again in the steamer entitled, so the soldiers said, to the Abyssinian War medal. He had seen his fellow elephants die of cold and epilepsy and starvation and sunstroke up at a place called Ali Musjid, ten years later; and afterward he had been sent down thousands of miles south to haul and pile big balks of teak in the timber yards at Moulmein. There he had half killed an insubordinate young elephant who was shirking his fair share of work.

After that he was taken off timber-hauling, and employed, with a few score other elephants who were trained to the business, in helping to catch wild elephants among the Garo hills. Elephants are very strictly managed by the Indian Government. There is one whole department which does nothing else but hunt them, and catch them, and break them in, and send them up and down the country as they are needed for work.

Kala Nag stood ten fair feet at the shoulders,
and his tusks had been cut off short at five feet,
and bound round the ends, to prevent them
splitting, with bands of copper; but he could do
more with those stumps than any untrained
elephant could do with the real sharpened ones.
When, after weeks and weeks of cautious driving
of scattered elephants across the hills, the forty or
fifty wild monsters were driven into the last
stockade, and the big drop gate, made of tree
trunks lashed together, jarred down behind them,
Kala Nag, at the word of command, would go
into that flaring, trumpeting pandemonium
(generally at night, when the flicker of the torches
made it difficult to judge distances), and, picking
out the biggest and wildest tusker of the mob,
would hammer him and hustle him into quiet
while the men on the backs of the other
elephants roped and tied the smaller ones.

There was nothing in the way of fighting that
Kala Nag, the old wise Black Snake, did not know,
for he had stood up more than once in his time
to the charge of the wounded tiger, and, curling

up his soft trunk to be out of harm's way, had knocked the springing brute sideways in mid-air with a quick sickle cut of his head, that he had invented all by himself; had knocked him over, and kneeled upon him with his huge knees till the life went out with a gasp and a howl, and there was only a fluffy striped thing on the ground for Kala Nag to pull by the tail.

"Yes," said Big Toomai, his driver, the son of Black Toomai who had taken him to Abyssinia, and grandson of Toomai of the Elephants who had seen him caught, "there is nothing that the Black Snake fears except me. He has seen three generations of us feed him and groom him, and he will live to see four."

"He is afraid of *me* also," said Little Toomai, standing up to his full height of four feet, with only one rag upon him. He was ten years old, the eldest son of Big Toomai, and, according to custom, he would take his father's place on Kala Nag's neck when he grew up, and would handle the heavy iron *ankus*, the elephant goad, that had been worn smooth by his father, and his grandfather, and his great-grandfather.

He knew what he was talking of; for he had been born under Kala Nag's shadow, had played with the end of his trunk before he could walk, had taken him down to water as soon as he could walk, and Kala Nag would no more have dreamed of disobeying his shrill little orders than he would have dreamed of killing him on that day when Big Toomai carried the little brown baby under Kala Nag's tusks, and told him to salute his master that was to be.

"Yes," said Little Toomai, "he is afraid of *me*," and he took long strides up to Kala Nag, called him a fat old pig, and made him lift up his feet one after the other.

"*Wah!*" said Little Toomai, "you are a big elephant," and he wagged his fluffy head, quoting his father. "The Government may pay for elephants, but they belong to us mahouts. When you are old, Kala Nag, there will come some rich rajah, and he will buy you from the Government, on account of your size and your manners, and then you will have nothing to do but to carry gold earrings in your ears, and a gold howdah on your back, and a red cloth covered with gold on

your sides, and walk at the head of the
processions of the King. Then I shall sit on your
neck, O Kala Nag, with a silver *ankus*, and men
will run before us with golden sticks, crying,
'Room for the King's elephant!' That will be good,
Kala Nag, but not so good as this hunting in the
jungles."

"*Umph!*" said Big Toomai. "You are a boy, and
as wild as a buffalo-calf. This running up and
down among the hills is not the best Government
service. I am getting old, and I do not love wild
elephants. Give me brick elephant lines, one stall
to each elephant, and big stumps to tie them to
safely, and flat, broad roads to exercise upon,
instead of this come-and-go camping. Aha, the
Cawnpore barracks were good. There was a
bazaar close by, and only three hours' work
a day."

Little Toomai remembered the Cawnpore
elephant lines and said nothing. He very much
preferred the camp life, and hated those broad,
flat roads, with the daily grubbing for grass in the
forage reserve, and the long hours when there was
nothing to do except to watch Kala Nag fidgeting

in his pickets.

What Little Toomai liked was to scramble up bridle paths that only an elephant could take; the dip into the valley below; the glimpses of the wild elephants browsing miles away; the rush of the frightened pig and peacock under Kala Nag's feet; the blinding warm rains, when all the hills and valleys smoked; the beautiful misty mornings when nobody knew where they would camp that night; the steady, cautious drive of the wild elephants, and the mad rush and blaze and hullabaloo of the last night's drive, when the elephants poured into the stockade like boulders in a landslide, found that they could not get out, and flung themselves at the heavy posts only to be driven back by yells and flaring torches and volleys of blank cartridge.

Even a little boy could be of use there, and Toomai was as useful as three boys. He would get his torch and wave it, and yell with the best. But the really good time came when the driving out began, and the *Keddah* – that is, the stockade – looked like a picture of the end of the world, and men had to make signs to one another, because they could not hear themselves speak. Then Little Toomai would climb up to the top of one of the quivering stockade posts, his sun-bleached brown hair flying loose all over his shoulders, and he looking like a goblin in the torchlight. And as soon as there was a lull you could hear his high-pitched yells of encouragement to Kala Nag, above the trumpeting and crashing, and snapping of ropes, and groans of the tethered elephants. "*Mail, mail, Kala Nag!* (Go on, go on, Black Snake!) *Dant do!* (Give him the tusk!) *Somalo! Somalo!* (Careful, careful!) *Maro! Mar!* (Hit him, hit him!) Mind the post! *Arré! Arré! Hai! Yai! Kya-a-ah!*" he would shout, and the big fight between Kala Nag and the wild elephant would sway to and fro across the *Keddah*, and the old elephant catchers would wipe the sweat out of their eyes, and find time to nod to Little Toomai wriggling with joy on the top of the posts.

He did more than wriggle. One night he slid down from the post and slipped in between the elephants and threw up the loose end of a rope, which had dropped, to a driver who was trying to get a purchase on the leg of a kicking young calf (calves always give more trouble than full-grown animals). Kala Nag saw him, caught him in his trunk, and handed him up to Big Toomai, who slapped him then and there, and put him back on the post.

Next morning he gave him a scolding and said, "Are not good brick elephant lines and a little tent carrying enough, that you must go elephant catching on your own account, little worthless? Now those foolish hunters, whose pay is less than my pay, have spoken to Petersen Sahib of the matter." Little Toomai was frightened. He did not know much of white men, but Petersen Sahib was the greatest white man in the world to him. He was the head of all the *Keddah* operations – the man who caught all the elephants for the Government of India, and who knew more about the ways of elephants than any living man.

"What – what will happen?" said Little Toomai.

"Happen! The worst that can happen. Petersen Sahib is a madman. Else why should he go hunting these wild devils? He may even require you to be an elephant catcher, to sleep anywhere in these fever-filled jungles, and at last to be trampled to death in the *Keddah*. It is well that this nonsense ends safely. Next week the catching is over, and we of the plains are sent back to our stations. Then we will march on smooth roads, and forget all this hunting. But, son, I am angry that you should meddle in the business that belongs to these Assamese jungle folk. Kala Nag will obey none but me, so I must go with him into the *Keddah*, but he is only a fighting elephant, and he does not help to rope them. So I sit at my ease, as befits a mahout, – not a mere hunter, – a mahout, I say, and a man who gets a pension at the end of his service. Is the family of Toomai of the Elephants to be trodden underfoot in the dirt of a *Keddah*? Bad one! Wicked one! Worthless son! Go and wash Kala Nag and attend to his ears, and see that there are no thorns in his feet. Or else Petersen Sahib will surely catch you and make you a wild hunter – a follower of elephant's foot tracks, a jungle bear. *Bah!* Shame! Go!"

Little Toomai went off without saying a word, but he told Kala Nag all his grievances while he was examining his feet. "No matter," said Little Toomai, turning up the fringe of Kala Nag's huge right ear. "They have said my name to Petersen Sahib, and perhaps – and perhaps – and perhaps – who knows? *Hai!* That is a big thorn that I have pulled out!"

The next few days were spent in getting the elephants together, in walking the newly caught wild elephants up and down between a couple of tame ones to prevent them giving too much trouble on the downward march to the plains, and in taking stock of the blankets and ropes and things that had been worn out or lost in the forest.

Petersen Sahib came in on his clever she-elephant Pudmini; he had been paying off other camps among the hills, for the season was coming to an end, and there was a clerk sitting at a table under a tree, to pay the drivers their wages. As each man was paid he went back to his elephant, and joined the line that stood ready to start. The catchers, and hunters, and beaters, the men of the regular *Keddah*, who stayed in the jungle year in and year out, sat on the backs of the elephants that belonged to Petersen Sahib's permanent force, or leaned against the trees with their guns across their arms, and made fun of the drivers who were going away, and laughed when the newly caught elephants broke the line and ran about.

Big Toomai went up to the clerk with Little Toomai behind him, and Machua Appa, the head tracker, said in an undertone to a friend of his, "There goes one piece of good elephant stuff at least. 'Tis a pity to send that young jungle-cock to moult in the plains."

Now Petersen Sahib had ears all over him, as a man must have who listens to the most silent of all living things – the wild elephant. He turned where he was lying all along on Pudmini's back and said, "What is that? I did not know of a man among the plains-drivers who had wit enough to rope even a dead elephant."

"This is not a man, but a boy. He went into the *Keddah* at the last drive, and threw Barmao there the rope, when we were trying to get that young calf with the blotch on his shoulder away from his mother."

Machua Appa pointed at Little Toomai, and Petersen Sahib looked, and Little Toomai bowed to the earth.

"He throw a rope? He is smaller than a picket pin. Little one, what is your name?" said Petersen Sahib.

Little Toomai was too frightened to speak, but Kala Nag was behind him, and Toomai made a sign with his hand, and the elephant caught him up in his trunk and held him level with Pudmini's forehead, in front of the great Petersen Sahib. Then Little Toomai covered his face with his hands, for he was only a child, and except where elephants were concerned, he was just as bashful as a child could be.

"Oho!" said Petersen Sahib, smiling underneath his moustache, "and why did you teach your elephant *that* trick? Was it to help you steal green corn from the roofs of the houses when the ears are put out to dry?"

"Not green corn, Protector of the Poor—melons," said Little Toomai, and all the men sitting about broke into a roar of laughter. Most of them had taught their elephants that trick when they were boys. Little Toomai was hanging eight feet up in the air, and he wished very much that he were eight feet underground.

"He is Toomai, my son, Sahib," said Big Toomai, scowling. "He is a very bad boy, and he will end in a jail, Sahib."

"Of that I have my doubts," said Petersen Sahib. "A boy who can face a full *Keddah* at his age does not end in jails. See, little one, here are four annas to spend in sweetmeats because you have a little head under that great thatch of hair. In time you may become a hunter too." Big Toomai scowled more than ever. "Remember, though, that *Keddahs* are not good for children to play in," Petersen Sahib went on.

"Must I never go there, Sahib?" asked Little Toomai with a big gasp.

"Yes." Petersen Sahib smiled again. "When you have seen the elephants dance. That is the proper time. Come to me when you have seen the elephants dance, and then I will let you go into all the *Keddahs*."

There was another roar of laughter, for that is an old joke among elephant-catchers, and it means just never. There are great cleared flat places hidden away in the forests that are called

elephants' ballrooms, but even these are only
found by accident, and no man has ever seen the
elephants dance. When a driver boasts of his skill
and bravery the other drivers say, "And when did
you see the elephants dance?"

Kala Nag put Little Toomai down, and he
bowed to the earth again and went away with his
father, and gave the silver four-anna piece to his
mother, who was nursing his baby brother, and
they all were put up on Kala Nag's back, and the
line of grunting, squealing elephants rolled down
the hill path to the plains. It was a very lively
march on account of the new elephants, who gave
trouble at every ford, and needed coaxing or
beating every other minute.

Big Toomai prodded Kala Nag spitefully, for he
was very angry, but Little Toomai was too happy
to speak. Petersen Sahib had noticed him, and
given him money, so he felt as a private soldier
would feel if he had been called out of the ranks
and praised by his commander-in-chief.

"What did Petersen Sahib mean by the
elephant dance?" he said, at last, softly to his
mother.

Big Toomai heard him and grunted. "That you should never be one of these hill buffaloes of trackers. *That* was what he meant. Oh, you in front, what is blocking the way?"

An Assamese driver, two or three elephants ahead, turned round angrily, crying: "Bring up Kala Nag, and knock this youngster of mine into good behaviour. Why should Petersen Sahib have chosen me to go down with you donkeys of the rice fields? Lay your beast alongside, Toomai, and let him prod with his tusks. By all the Gods of the Hills, these new elephants are possessed, or else they can smell their companions in the jungle." Kala Nag hit the new elephant in the ribs and knocked the wind out of him, as Big Toomai said, "We have swept the hills of wild elephants at the last catch. It is only your carelessness in driving. Must I keep order along the whole line?"

"Hear him!" said the other driver. "*We* have swept the hills! Ho! Ho! You are very wise, you plains people. Anyone but a mud-head who never saw the jungle would know that *they* know that the drives are ended for the season. Therefore all the wild elephants tonight will – but why should

I waste wisdom on a river turtle?"

"What will they do?" Little Toomai called out.

"*Ohé*, little one. Are you there? Well, I will tell you, for you have a cool head. They will dance, and your father, who has swept *all* the hills of *all* the elephants, would do well to double-chain his pickets tonight."

"What talk is this?" said Big Toomai. "For forty years, father and son, we have tended elephants, and we have never heard such moonshine about dances."

"Yes; but a plainsman who lives in a hut knows only the four walls of his hut. Well, leave your elephants unshackled tonight and see what comes. As for their dancing, I have seen the place where – *Bapree-bap!* How many windings has the Dihang River? Here is another ford, and we must swim the calves. Stop still, you behind there!"

And in this way, talking and wrangling and splashing through the rivers, they made their first march to a sort of receiving camp for the new elephants. But they lost their tempers long before they got there.

Then the elephants were chained by their hind

legs to their big stumps of pickets, and extra ropes were fitted to the new elephants, and the fodder was piled before them, and the hill drivers went back to Petersen Sahib through the afternoon light, telling the plains drivers to be extra careful that night, and laughing when the plains drivers asked the reason.

Little Toomai attended to Kala Nag's supper, and as evening fell, wandered through the camp, unspeakably happy, in search of a tom-tom. When an Indian child's heart is full, he does not run about and make a noise in an irregular fashion. He sits down to a sort of revel all by himself. And Little Toomai had been spoken to by Petersen Sahib! If he had not found what he wanted, I believe he would have been ill. But the sweetmeat seller in the camp lent him a little tom-tom – a drum beaten with the flat of the hand – and he sat down, cross-legged, before Kala Nag as the stars began to come out, the tom-tom in his lap, and he thumped and he thumped and he thumped, and the more he thought of the great honour that had been done to him, the more he thumped, all alone among the elephant fodder. There was no tune and no words, but the thumping made him happy.

The new elephants strained at their ropes, and squealed and trumpeted from time to time, and he could hear his mother in the camp hut putting his small brother to sleep with an old, old song about the great God Shiv, who once told all the animals what they should eat. It is a very soothing lullaby, and the first verse says:

Shiv, who poured the harvest and made the winds to blow,
Sitting at the doorways of a day of long ago,
Gave to each his portion, food and toil and fate,
From the King upon the cushion to the Beggar at the gate.
All things made he – Shiva the Preserver.
Mahadeo! Mahadeo! He made all –
Thorn for the camel, fodder for the kine,
And mother's heart for sleepy head, O little son of mine!

Little Toomai came in with a joyous tunk-a-tunk at the end of each verse, till he felt sleepy and stretched himself on the fodder at Kala Nag's side. At last the elephants began to lie down one after another as is their custom, till only Kala

Nag at the right of the line was left standing up; and he rocked slowly from side to side, his ears put forward to listen to the night wind as it blew very slowly across the hills. The air was full of all the night noises that, taken together, make one big silence – the click of one bamboo stem against the other, the rustle of something alive in the undergrowth, the scratch and squawk of a half-waked bird (birds are awake in the night much more often than we imagine), and the fall of water ever so far away. Little Toomai slept for some time, and when he waked it was brilliant moonlight, and Kala Nag was still standing up with his ears cocked. Little Toomai turned, rustling in the fodder, and watched the curve of his big back against half the stars in heaven, and while he watched he heard, so far away that it sounded no more than a pinhole of noise pricked through the stillness, the *"hoot-toot"* of a wild elephant.

All the elephants in the lines jumped up as if they had been shot, and their grunts at last waked the sleeping mahouts, and they came out and drove in the picket pegs with big mallets, and tightened this rope and knotted that till all was quiet. One new elephant had nearly grubbed up his picket, and Big Toomai took off Kala Nag's leg chain and shackled that elephant fore-foot to hind-foot, but slipped a loop of grass string round Kala Nag's leg, and told him to remember that he was tied fast. He knew that he and his father and his grandfather had done the very same thing hundreds of times before. Kala Nag did not answer to the order by gurgling, as he usually did. He stood still, looking out across the moonlight, his head a little raised and his ears spread like fans, up to the great folds of the Garo hills.

"Tend to him if he grows restless in the night," said Big Toomai to Little Toomai, and he went into the hut and slept. Little Toomai was just going to sleep, too, when he heard the coir string snap with a little "tang," and Kala Nag rolled out of his pickets as slowly and as silently as a cloud rolls out of the mouth of a valley. Little Toomai pattered after him, barefooted, down the road in the moonlight, calling under his breath, "Kala Nag! Kala Nag! Take me with you, O Kala Nag!" The elephant turned, without a sound, took three strides back to the boy in the moonlight, put down his trunk, swung him up to his neck, and almost before Little Toomai had settled his knees, slipped into the forest.

There was one blast of furious trumpeting from the lines, and then the silence shut down on everything, and Kala Nag began to move. Sometimes a tuft of high grass washed along his sides as a wave washes along the sides of a ship, and sometimes a cluster of wild-pepper vines would scrape along his back, or a bamboo would creak where his shoulder touched it. But between those times he moved absolutely without any sound, drifting through the thick Garo forest as though it had been smoke. He was going uphill, but though Little Toomai watched the stars in the rifts of the trees, he could not tell in what direction.

Then Kala Nag reached the crest of the ascent and stopped for a minute, and Little Toomai could see the tops of the trees lying all speckled and furry under the moonlight for miles and miles, and the blue-white mist over the river in the hollow. Toomai leaned forward and looked, and he felt that the forest was awake below him – awake and alive and crowded. A big brown fruit-eating bat brushed past his ear; a porcupine's quills rattled in the thicket; and in the darkness between the tree stems he heard a hog bear digging hard in the moist warm earth, and snuffing as it digged.

Then the branches closed over his head again, and Kala Nag began to go down into the valley – not quietly this time, but as a runaway gun goes down a steep bank – in one rush. The huge limbs moved as steadily as pistons, eight feet to each stride, and the wrinkled skin of the elbow points rustled. The undergrowth on either side of him ripped with a noise like torn canvas, and the saplings that he heaved away right and left with his shoulders sprang back again and banged him on the flank, and great trails of creepers, all matted together, hung from his tusks as he threw his head from side to side and ploughed out his pathway. Then Little Toomai laid himself down close to the great neck lest a swinging bough should sweep him to the ground, and he wished that he were back in the lines again.

The grass began to get squashy, and Kala Nag's feet sucked and squelched as he put them down, and the night mist at the bottom of the valley chilled Little Toomai. There was a splash and a trample, and the rush of running water, and Kala Nag strode through the bed of a river, feeling his way at each step. Above the noise of the water, as it swirled round the elephant's legs, Little Toomai could hear more splashing and some trumpeting both upstream and down – great grunts and angry snortings, and all the mist about him seemed to be full of rolling, wavy shadows.

"*Ai!*" he said, half aloud, his teeth chattering. "The elephant-folk are out tonight. It is the dance, then!"

Kala Nag swashed out of the water, blew his trunk clear, and began another climb. But this time he was not alone, and he had not to make his path. That was made already, six feet wide, in front of him, where the bent jungle grass was trying to recover itself and stand up. Many elephants must have gone that way only a few minutes before. Little Toomai looked back, and behind him a great wild tusker with his little pig's eyes glowing like hot coals was just lifting himself out of the misty river. Then the trees closed up again, and they went on and up, with trumpetings and crashings, and the sound of breaking branches on every side of them.

At last Kala Nag stood still between two tree trunks at the very top of the hill. They were part of a circle of trees that grew round an irregular space of some three or four acres, and in all that space, as Little Toomai could see, the ground had been trampled down as hard as a brick floor. Some trees grew in the centre of the clearing, but their bark was rubbed away, and the white wood beneath showed all shiny and polished in the patches of moonlight. There were creepers hanging from the upper branches, and the bells of the flowers of the creepers, great waxy white things like convolvuluses, hung down fast asleep. But within the limits of the clearing there was not a single blade of green – nothing but the trampled earth.

The moonlight showed it all iron grey, except where some elephants stood upon it, and their shadows were inky black. Little Toomai looked, holding his breath, with his eyes starting out of his head, and as he looked, more and more and more elephants swung out into the open from between the tree trunks. Little Toomai could only count up to ten, and he counted again and again on his fingers till he lost count of the tens, and his head began to swim. Outside the clearing he could hear them crashing in the undergrowth as they worked their way up the hillside, but as soon as they were within the circle of the tree trunks they moved like ghosts.

There were white-tusked wild males, with fallen leaves and nuts and twigs lying in the wrinkles of their necks and the folds of their ears; fat, slow-footed she-elephants, with restless, little pinky black calves only three or four feet high running under their stomachs; young elephants with their tusks just beginning to show, and very proud of them; lanky, scraggy old-maid elephants, with their hollow anxious faces, and trunks like rough bark; savage old bull elephants, scarred from shoulder to flank with great weals and cuts of bygone fights, and the caked dirt of their solitary mud baths dropping from their

shoulders; and there was one with a broken tusk and the marks of the full stroke, the terrible drawing scrape, of a tiger's claws on his side.

They were standing head to head, or walking to and fro across the ground in couples, or rocking and swaying all by themselves – scores and scores of elephants.

Toomai knew that so long as he lay still on Kala Nag's neck nothing would happen to him, for even in the rush and scramble of a *Keddah* drive a wild elephant does not reach up with his trunk and drag a man off the neck of a tame elephant. And these elephants were not thinking of men that night. Once they started and put their ears forward when they heard the chinking of a leg iron in the forest, but it was Pudmini, Petersen Sahib's pet elephant, her chain snapped short off, grunting, snuffling up the hillside. She must have broken her pickets and come straight from Petersen Sahib's camp; and Little Toomai saw another elephant, one that he did not know, with deep rope galls on his back and breast. He, too, must have run away from some camp in the hills about.

At last there was no sound of any more elephants moving in the forest, and Kala Nag rolled out from his station between the trees and went into the middle of the crowd, clucking and gurgling, and all the elephants began to talk in their own tongue, and to move about.

Still lying down, Little Toomai looked down upon scores and scores of broad backs, and wagging ears, and tossing trunks, and little rolling eyes. He heard the click of tusks as they crossed other tusks by accident, and the dry rustle of trunks twined together, and the chafing of enormous sides and shoulders in the crowd, and the incessant flick and *hissh* of the great tails. Then a cloud came over the moon, and he sat in black darkness. But the quiet, steady hustling and pushing and gurgling went on just the same. He knew that there were elephants all round Kala Nag, and that there was no chance of backing him out of the assembly; so he set his teeth and shivered. In a *Keddah* at least there was torchlight and shouting, but here he was all alone in the dark, and once a trunk came up and touched him on the knee.

Then an elephant trumpeted, and they all took it up for five or ten terrible seconds. The dew from the trees above spattered down like rain on the unseen backs, and a dull booming noise began, not very loud at first, and Little Toomai could not tell what it was. But it grew and grew, and Kala Nag lifted up one forefoot and then the other, and brought them down on the ground – one-two, one-two, as steadily as triphammers. The elephants were stamping all together now, and it sounded like a war drum beaten at the mouth of a cave. The dew fell from the trees till there was no more left to fall, and the booming went on, and the ground rocked and shivered, and Little Toomai put his hands up to his ears to shut out the sound. But it was all one gigantic jar that ran through him – this stamp of hundreds of heavy feet on the raw earth. Once or twice he could feel Kala Nag and all the others surge forward a few strides, and the thumping would change to the crushing sound of juicy green things being bruised, but in a minute or two the boom of feet on hard earth began again. A tree was creaking and groaning somewhere near him. He put out his arm and felt the bark, but Kala Nag moved forward, still tramping, and he could not tell where he was in the clearing. There was no sound from the elephants, except once, when two or three little calves squeaked together. Then he heard a thump and a shuffle, and the booming went on. It must have lasted fully two hours, and Little Toomai ached in every nerve, but he knew by the smell of the night air that the dawn was coming.

The morning broke in one sheet of pale yellow behind the green hills, and the booming stopped with the first ray, as though the light had been an order. Before Little Toomai had got the ringing out of his head, before even he had shifted his position, there was not an elephant in sight except Kala Nag, Pudmini, and the elephant with the rope-galls, and there was neither sign nor rustle nor whisper down the hillsides to show where the others had gone.

Little Toomai stared again and again. The clearing, as he remembered it, had grown bigger in the night. More trees stood in the middle of it, but the undergrowth and the jungle grass at the sides had been rolled back. Little Toomai stared once more. Now he understood the trampling. The elephants had stamped out more room – had stamped the thick grass and juicy cane to trash, the trash into slivers, the slivers into tiny fibres, and the fibres into hard earth.

"*Wah!*" said Little Toomai, and his eyes were very heavy. "Kala Nag, my lord, let us keep by Pudmini and go to Petersen Sahib's camp, or I shall drop from your neck."

The third elephant watched the two go away, snorted, wheeled round, and took his own path. He may have belonged to some little king's establishment, fifty or sixty or a hundred miles away.

Two hours later, as Petersen Sahib was eating early breakfast, his elephants, who had been double chained that night, began to trumpet, and Pudmini, mired to the shoulders, with Kala Nag, very footsore, shambled into the camp. Little Toomai's face was grey and pinched, and his hair was full of leaves and drenched with dew, but he tried to salute Petersen Sahib, and cried faintly: "The dance – the elephant dance! I have seen it, and – I die!" As Kala Nag sat down, he slid off his neck in a dead faint.

But, since Indian children have no nerves worth speaking of, in two hours he was lying very contentedly in Petersen Sahib's hammock with Petersen Sahib's shooting coat under his head, and a glass of warm milk, a little brandy, with a dash of quinine, inside of him, and while the old hairy, scarred hunters of the jungles sat three deep before him, looking at him as though he were a spirit, he told his tale in short words, as a child will, and wound up with:

"Now, if I lie in one word, send men to see, and they will find that the elephant folk have trampled down more room in their dance room, and they will find ten and ten, and many times ten, tracks leading to that dance-room. They made more room with their feet. I have seen it. Kala Nag took me, and I saw. Also Kala Nag is very leg-weary!"

Little Toomai lay back and slept all through the long afternoon and into the twilight, and while he slept Petersen Sahib and Machua Appa followed the track of the two elephants for

fifteen miles across the hills. Petersen Sahib had
spent eighteen years in catching elephants, and he
had only once before found such a dance place.
Machua Appa had no need to look twice at the
clearing to see what had been done there, or to
scratch with his toe in the packed, rammed earth.

"The child speaks truth," said he. "All this was
done last night, and I have counted seventy tracks
crossing the river. See, Sahib, where Pudmini's
leg-iron cut the bark of that tree! Yes; she was
there too."

They looked at one another and up and down,
and they wondered. For the ways of elephants are
beyond the wit of any man, black or white, to
fathom.

"Forty years and five," said Machua Appa, "have
I followed my lord, the elephant, but never have I
heard that any child of man had seen what this
child has seen. By all the Gods of the Hills, it is
– what can we say?" and he shook his head.

When they got back to camp it was time for
the evening meal. Petersen Sahib ate alone in his
tent, but he gave orders that the camp should
have two sheep and some fowls, as well as a

double ration of flour and rice and salt, for he
knew that there would be a feast.

Big Toomai had come up hotfoot from the
camp in the plains to search for his son and his
elephant, and now that he had found them he
looked at them as though he were afraid of them
both. And there was a feast by the blazing
campfires in front of the lines of picketed
elephants, and Little Toomai was the hero of it all.
And the big brown elephant catchers, the trackers
and drivers and ropers, and the men who know
all the secrets of breaking the wildest elephants,
passed him from one to the other, and they
marked his forehead with blood from the breast
of a newly killed jungle-cock, to show that he was
a forester, initiated and free of all the jungles.

And at last, when the flames died down, and
the red light of the logs made the elephants look
as though they had been dipped in blood too,
Machua Appa, the head of all the drivers of all
the *Keddahs* – Machua Appa, Petersen Sahib's other
self, who had never seen a made road in forty
years: Machua Appa, who was so great that he
had no other name than Machua Appa, – leaped

to his feet, with Little Toomai held high in the air above his head, and shouted: "Listen, my brothers. Listen, too, you my lords in the lines there, for I, Machua Appa, am speaking! This little one shall no more be called Little Toomai, but Toomai of the Elephants, as his great-grandfather was called before him. What never man has seen he has seen through the long night, and the favour of the elephant-folk and of the Gods of the Jungles is with him. He shall become a great tracker. He shall become greater than I, even I, Machua Appa! He shall follow the new trail, and the stale trail, and the mixed trail, with a clear eye! He shall take no harm in the *Keddah* when he runs under their bellies to rope the wild tuskers; and if he slips before the feet of the charging bull elephant, the bull elephant shall know who he is and shall not crush him. *Aihai!* my lords in the chains," – he whirled up the line of pickets – "here is the little one that has seen your dances in your hidden places, – the sight that never man saw! Give him honour, my lords! *Salaam karo*, my children. Make your salute to Toomai of the Elephants! Gunga Pershad, ahaa! Hira Guj, Birchi Guj, Kuttar Guj, *ahaa!* Pudmini, – you have seen him at the dance, and you too, Kala Nag, my pearl among elephants! *Ahaa!* Together! To Toomai of the Elephants. *Barrao!*"

And at that last wild yell the whole line flung up their trunks till the tips touched their foreheads, and broke out into the full salute – the crashing trumpet-peal that only the Viceroy of India hears, the Salaamut of the *Keddah*.

But it was all for the sake of Little Toomai, who had seen what never man had seen before – the dance of the elephants at night and alone in the heart of the Garo hills!

SHIV AND THE GRASSHOPPER
(The song that Toomai's mother sang to the baby)

Shiv, who poured the harvest and made the winds to blow,
Sitting at the doorways of a day of long ago,
Gave to each his portion, food and toil and fate,
From the King upon the cushion to the Beggar at the gate.
All things made he – Shiva the Preserver.
Mahadeo! Mahadeo! He made all –
Thorn for the camel, fodder for the kine,
And mother's heart for sleepy head,
O little son of mine!
Wheat he gave to rich folk, millet to the poor,
Broken scraps for holy men that beg from door to door;
Cattle to the tiger, carrion to the kite,
And rags and bones to wicked wolves outside the wall at night.
Naught he found too lofty, none he saw too low –
Parvati beside him watched them come and go;
Thought to cheat her husband, turning Shiv to jest –
Stole the little grasshopper and hid it in her breast.

So she tricked him, Shiva the Preserver.
Mahadeo! Mahadeo! Turn and see.
Tall are the camels, heavy are the kine,
But this was Least of Little Things,
O little son of mine!
When the dole was ended, laughingly she said,
"Master, of a million mouths, is not one unfed?"
Laughing, Shiv made answer, "All have had their part,
Even he, the little one, hidden 'neath thy heart."
From her breast she plucked it, Parvati the thief,
Saw the Least of Little Things gnawed a new-grown leaf!
Saw and feared and wondered, making prayer to Shiv,
Who hath surely given meat to all that live.
All things made he – Shiva the Preserver.
Mahadeo! Mahadeo! He made all,–
Thorn for the camel, fodder for the kine,
And mother's heart for sleepy head,
O little son of mine!

Her Majesty's Servants

You can work it out by Fractions or by simple Rule of Three,
But the way of Tweedledum is not the way of Tweedledee.
You can twist it, you can turn it, you can plait it till you drop,
But the way of Pilly Winky's not the way of Winkie Pop!

IT had been raining heavily for one whole month – raining on a camp of thirty thousand men and thousands of camels, elephants, horses, bullocks, and mules all gathered together at a place called Rawal Pindi, to be reviewed by the Viceroy of India. He was receiving a visit from the Amir of Afghanistan – a wild king of a very wild country. The Amir had brought with him for a bodyguard eight hundred men and horses who had never seen a camp or a locomotive before in their lives – savage men and savage horses from somewhere at the back of Central Asia. Every night a mob of these horses would be sure to break their heel ropes and stampede up and down the camp through the mud in the dark, or the camels would break loose and run about and fall over the ropes of the tents, and you can imagine how pleasant that was for men trying to go to sleep. My tent lay far away from the camel lines, and I thought it was safe. But one night a man popped his head in and shouted, "Get out, quick! They're coming! My tent's gone!"

I knew who 'they' were, so I put on my boots

and waterproof and scuttled out into the slush. Little Vixen, my fox terrier, went out through the other side; and then there was a roaring and a grunting and bubbling, and I saw the tent cave in, as the pole snapped, and begin to dance about like a mad ghost. A camel had blundered into it, and wet and angry as I was, I could not help laughing. Then I ran on, because I did not know how many camels might have got loose, and before long I was out of sight of the camp, ploughing my way through the mud.

At last I fell over the tail-end of a gun, and by that knew I was somewhere near the artillery lines where the cannon were stacked at night. As I did not want to plowter about any more in the drizzle and the dark, I put my waterproof over the muzzle of one gun, and made a sort of wigwam with two or three rammers that I found, and lay along the tail of another gun, wondering where Vixen had got to, and where I might be.

Just as I was getting ready to go to sleep I heard a jingle of harness and a grunt, and a mule passed me shaking his wet ears. He belonged to a screw-gun battery, for I could hear the rattle of the straps and rings and chains and things on his saddle pad. The screw-guns are tiny little cannon made in two pieces, that are screwed together when the time comes to use them. They are taken up mountains, anywhere that a mule can find a road, and they are very useful for fighting in rocky country.

Behind the mule there was a camel, with his big soft feet squelching and slipping in the mud, and his neck bobbing to and fro like a strayed hen's. Luckily, I knew enough of beast language – not wild-beast language, but camp-beast language, of course – to know what he was saying.

He must have been the one that flopped into my tent, for he called to the mule, "What shall I do? Where shall I go? I have fought with a white thing that waved, and it took a stick and hit me on the neck." (That was my broken tent pole, and I was very glad to know it.) "Shall we run on?"

"Oh, it was you," said the mule, "you and your friends, that have been disturbing the camp? All right. You'll be beaten for this in the morning. But I may as well give you something on account now."

I heard the harness jingle as the mule backed and caught the camel two kicks in the ribs that rang like a drum. "Another time," he said, "you'll know better than to run through a mule battery at night, shouting 'Thieves and fire!' Sit down, and keep your silly neck quiet."

The camel doubled up camel-fashion, like a two-foot rule, and sat down whimpering. There was a regular beat of hoofs in the darkness, and a big troop horse cantered up as steadily as though he were on parade, jumped a gun tail, and landed close to the mule.

"It's disgraceful," he said, blowing out his nostrils. "Those camels have racketed through our lines again – the third time this week. How's a horse to keep his condition if he isn't allowed to sleep. Who's here?"

"I'm the breech-piece mule of number two gun of the First Screw Battery," said the mule, "and the other's one of your friends. He's waked me up too. Who are you?"

"Number Fifteen, E troop, Ninth Lancers – Dick Cunliffe's horse. Stand over a little, there."

"Oh, beg your pardon," said the mule. "It's too

dark to see much. Aren't these camels too sickening for anything? I walked out of my lines to get a little peace and quiet here."

"My lords," said the camel humbly, "we dreamed bad dreams in the night, and we were very much afraid. I am only a baggage camel of the 39th Native Infantry, and I am not as brave as you are, my lords."

"Then why didn't you stay and carry baggage for the 39th Native Infantry, instead of running all round the camp?" said the mule.

"They were such very bad dreams," said the camel. "I am sorry. Listen! What is that? Shall we run on again?"

"Sit down," said the mule, "or you'll snap your long stick legs between the guns." He cocked one ear and listened. "Bullocks!" he said. "Gun bullocks. On my word, you and your friends have waked the camp very thoroughly. It takes a good deal of prodding to put up a gun bullock."

I heard a chain dragging along the ground, and a yoke of the great sulky white bullocks that drag the heavy siege guns when the elephants won't go any nearer to the firing, came shouldering along

together. And almost stepping on the chain was another battery mule, calling wildly for "Billy."

"That's one of our recruits," said the old mule to the troop horse. "He's calling for me. Here, youngster, stop squealing. The dark never hurt anybody yet."

The gun bullocks lay down together and began chewing the cud, but the young mule huddled close to Billy.

"Things!" he said. "Fearful and horrible, Billy! They came into our lines while we were asleep. D'you think they'll kill us?"

"I've a very great mind to give you a number one kicking," said Billy. "The idea of a fourteen-hand mule with your training disgracing the battery before this gentleman!"

"Gently, gently!" said the troop horse. "Remember they are always like this to begin with. The first time I ever saw a man (it was in Australia when I was a three year old) I ran for half a day, and if I'd seen a camel, I should have been running still."

Nearly all our horses for the English cavalry are brought to India from Australia, and are broken in by the troopers themselves.

"True enough," said Billy. "Stop shaking, youngster. The first time they put the full harness with all its chains on my back I stood on my forelegs and kicked every bit of it off. I hadn't learned the *real* science of kicking then, but the battery said they had never seen anything like it."

"But this wasn't harness or anything that jingled," said the young mule. "You know I don't mind that now, Billy. It was Things like trees, and they fell up and down the lines and bubbled; and my head-rope broke, and I couldn't find my driver, and I couldn't find you, Billy, so I ran off with – with these gentlemen."

"*Hm!*" said Billy. "As soon as I heard the camels were loose I came away on my own account. When a battery – a screw-gun mule calls gun bullocks gentlemen, he must be very badly shaken up. Who are you fellows on the ground there?"

The gun bullocks rolled their cuds, and answered both together: "The seventh yoke of the first gun of the Big Gun Battery. We were asleep when the camels came, but when we were trampled on we got up and walked away. It is better to lie quiet in the mud than to be disturbed on good bedding. We told your friend here that there was nothing to be afraid of, but he knew so much that he thought otherwise. *Wah!*"

They went on chewing.

"That comes of being afraid," said Billy. "You get laughed at by gun bullocks. I hope you like it, young un."

The young mule's teeth snapped, and I heard him say something about not being afraid of any beefy old bullock in the world. But the bullocks only clicked their horns together and went on chewing.

"Now, don't be angry after you've been afraid. That's the worst kind of cowardice," said the troop horse. "Anybody can be forgiven for being scared in the night, I think, if they see things they don't understand. We've broken out of our pickets, again and again, four hundred and fifty of us, just because a new recruit got to telling tales of whip snakes at home in Australia till we were scared to death of the loose ends of our head ropes."

"That's all very well in camp," said Billy. "I'm

not above stampeding myself, for the fun of the thing, when I haven't been out for a day or two. But what do you do on active service?"

"Oh, that's quite another set of new shoes," said the troop horse. "Dick Cunliffe's on my back then, and drives his knees into me, and all I have to do is to watch where I am putting my feet, and to keep my hind legs well under me, and be bridle-wise."

"What's bridle-wise?" said the young mule.

"By the Blue Gums of the Back Blocks," snorted the troop horse, "do you mean to say that you aren't taught to be bridle-wise in your business? How can you do anything, unless you can spin round at once when the rein is pressed on your neck? It means life or death to your man, and of course that's life and death to you. Get round with your hind legs under you the instant you feel the rein on your neck. If you haven't room to swing round, rear up a little and come round on your hind legs. That's being bridle-wise."

"We aren't taught that way," said Billy the mule stiffly. "We're taught to obey the man at our head: step off when he says so, and step in when he says so. I suppose it comes to the same thing. Now, with all this fine fancy business and rearing, which must be very bad for your hocks, what do you *do*?"

"That depends," said the troop horse. "Generally I have to go in among a lot of yelling, hairy men with knives – long shiny knives, worse than the farrier's knives – and I have to take care that Dick's boot is just touching the next man's boot without crushing it. I can see Dick's lance to the right of my right eye, and I know I'm safe. I shouldn't care to be the man or horse that stood up to Dick and me when we're in a hurry."

"Don't the knives hurt?" said the young mule.

"Well, I got one cut across the chest once, but that wasn't Dick's fault –"

"A lot I should have cared whose fault it was, if it hurt!" said the young mule.

"You must," said the troop horse. "If you don't trust your man, you may as well run away at once. That's what some of our horses do, and I don't blame them. As I was saying, it wasn't Dick's fault. The man was lying on the ground, and I stretched myself not to tread on him, and he slashed up at me. Next time I have to go over a man lying down I shall step on him – hard."

"*Hm!*" said Billy. "It sounds very foolish. Knives are dirty things at any time. The proper thing to do is to climb up a mountain with a well-balanced saddle, hang on by all four feet and your ears too, and creep and crawl and wriggle along, till you come out hundreds of feet above anyone else on a ledge where there's just room enough for your hoofs. Then you stand still and keep quiet – never ask a man to hold your head, young un – keep quiet while the guns are being put together, and then you watch the little poppy shells drop down into the treetops ever so far below."

"Don't you ever trip?" said the troop horse.

"They say that when a mule trips you can split a hen's ear," said Billy. "Now and again *perhaps* a badly packed saddle will upset a mule, but it's very seldom. I wish I could show you our business. It's beautiful. Why, it took me three years to find out what the men were driving at. The science of the thing is never to show up against the skyline, because, if you do, you may get fired at. Remember that, young un. Always keep hidden as much as possible, even if you have to go a mile out of your way. I lead the battery when it comes to that sort of climbing."

"Fired at without the chance of running into the people who are firing!" said the troop horse, thinking hard. "I couldn't stand that. I should want to charge – with Dick."

"Oh, no, you wouldn't. You know that as soon as the guns are in position *they'll* do all the charging. That's scientific and neat. But knives – *pah!*"

The baggage camel had been bobbing his head to and fro for some time past, anxious to get a word in edgewise. Then I heard him say, as he cleared his throat, nervously:

"I – I – I have fought a little, but not in that climbing way or that running way."

"No. Now you mention it," said Billy, "you don't look as though you were made for climbing or running – much. Well, how was it, old Hay-bales?"

"The proper way," said the camel. "We all sat down –"

"Oh, my crupper and breastplate!" said the

troop horse under his breath. "Sat down!"

"We sat down – a hundred of us," the camel went on, "in a big square, and the men piled our *kajawahs*, our packs and saddles, outside the square, and they fired over our backs, the men did, on all sides of the square."

"What sort of men? Any men that came along?" said the troop horse. "They teach us in riding school to lie down and let our masters fire across us, but Dick Cunliffe is the only man I'd trust to do that. It tickles my girths, and, besides, I can't see with my head on the ground."

"What does it matter who fires across you?" said the camel. "There are plenty of men and plenty of other camels close by, and a great many clouds of smoke. I am not frightened then. I sit still and wait."

"And yet," said Billy, "you dream bad dreams and upset the camp at night. Well, well! Before I'd lie down, not to speak of sitting down, and let a man fire across me, my heels and his head would have something to say to each other. Did you ever hear anything so awful as that?"

There was a long silence, and then one of the

gun bullocks lifted up his big head and said, "This is very foolish indeed. There is only one way of fighting."

"Oh, go on," said Billy. "*Please* don't mind me. I suppose you fellows fight standing on your tails?"

"Only one way," said the two together. (They must have been twins.) "This is that way. To put all twenty yoke of us to the big gun as soon as Two Tails trumpets." ('Two Tails' is camp slang for the elephant.)

"What does Two Tails trumpet for?" said the young mule.

"To show that he is not going any nearer to the smoke on the other side. Two Tails is a great coward. Then we tug the big gun all together – *Heya – Hullah! Heeyah! Hullah! We* do not climb like cats nor run like calves. We go across the level plain, twenty yoke of us, till we are unyoked again, and we graze while the big guns talk across the plain to some town with mud walls, and pieces of the wall fall out, and the dust goes up as though many cattle were coming home."

"Oh! And you choose that time for grazing?" said the young mule.

"That time or any other. Eating is always good. We eat till we are yoked up again and tug the gun back to where Two Tails is waiting for it. Sometimes there are big guns in the city that speak back, and some of us are killed, and then there is all the more grazing for those that are left. This is Fate. None the less, Two Tails is a great coward. That is the proper way to fight. We are brothers from Hapur. Our father was a sacred bull of Shiva. We have spoken."

"Well, I've certainly learned something tonight," said the troop horse. "Do you gentlemen of the screw-gun battery feel inclined to eat when you are being fired at with big guns, and Two Tails is behind you?"

"About as much as we feel inclined to sit down and let men sprawl all over us, or run into people with knives. I never heard such stuff. A mountain ledge, a well-balanced load, a driver you can trust to let you pick your own way, and I'm your mule. But – the other things – no!" said Billy, with a stamp of his foot.

"Of course," said the troop horse, "everyone is not made in the same way, and I can quite see

that your family, on your father's side, would fail
to understand a great many things."

"Never you mind my family on my father's
side," said Billy angrily, for every mule hates to be
reminded that his father was a donkey. "My
father was a Southern gentleman, and he could
pull down and bite and kick into rags every horse
he came across. Remember that, you big brown
Brumby!"

Brumby means wild horse without any
breeding. You can imagine how the Australian
horse felt. I saw the white of his eye glitter in
the dark.

"See here, you son of an imported Malaga
jackass," he said between his teeth, "I'd have you
know that I'm related on my mother's side to
Carbine, winner of the Melbourne Cup, and
where I come from we aren't accustomed to
being ridden over roughshod by any parrot-
mouthed, pig-headed mule in a popgun
peashooter battery. Are you ready?"

"On your hind legs!" squealed Billy. They both
reared up facing each other, and I was expecting
a furious fight, when a gurgly, rumbly voice,

called out of the darkness to the right – "Children, what are you fighting about there? Be quiet."

Both beasts dropped down with a snort of disgust, for neither horse nor mule can bear to listen to an elephant's voice.

"It's Two Tails!" said the troop horse. "I can't stand him. A tail at each end isn't fair!"

"My feelings exactly," said Billy, crowding into the troop horse for company. "We're very alike in some things."

"I suppose we've inherited them from our mothers," said the troop horse. "It's not worth quarrelling about. Hi! Two Tails, are you tied up?"

"Yes," said Two Tails, with a laugh all up his trunk. "I'm picketed for the night. I've heard what you fellows have been saying. But don't be afraid. I'm not coming over."

The bullocks and the camel said, half aloud, "Afraid of Two Tails – what nonsense!" And the bullocks went on, "We are sorry that you heard, but it is true. Two Tails, why are you afraid of the guns when they fire?"

"Well," said Two Tails, rubbing one hind leg against the other, exactly like a little boy saying a poem, "I don't quite know whether you'd understand."

"We don't, but we have to pull the guns," said the bullocks.

"I know it, and I know you are a good deal braver than you think you are. But it's different with me. My battery captain called me a Pachydermatous Anachronism the other day."

"That's another way of fighting, I suppose?" said Billy, who was recovering his spirits.

"*You* don't know what that means, of course, but I do. It means betwixt and between, and that is just where I am. I can see inside my head what will happen when a shell bursts, and you bullocks can't."

"I can," said the troop horse. "At least a little bit. I try not to think about it."

"I can see more than you, and I do think about it. I know there's a great deal of me to take care of, and I know that nobody knows how to cure me when I'm sick. All they can do is to stop my driver's pay till I get well, and I can't trust my driver."

"Ah!" said the troop horse. "That explains it. I

can trust Dick."

"You could put a whole regiment of Dicks on my back without making me feel any better. I know just enough to be uncomfortable, and not enough to go on in spite of it."

"We do not understand," said the bullocks.

"I know you don't. I'm not talking to you. You don't know what blood is."

"We do," said the bullocks. "It is red stuff that soaks into the ground and smells."

The troop horse gave a kick and a bound and a snort.

"Don't talk of it," he said. "I can smell it now, just thinking of it. It makes me want to run – when I haven't Dick on my back."

"But it is not here," said the camel and the bullocks. "Why are you so stupid?"

"It's vile stuff," said Billy. "I don't want to run, but I don't want to talk about it."

"There you are!" said Two Tails, waving his tail to explain.

"Surely. Yes, we have been here all night," said the bullocks.

Two Tails stamped his foot till the iron ring on

it jingled. "Oh, I'm not talking to *you*. You can't see inside your heads."

"No. We see out of our four eyes," said the bullocks. "We see straight in front of us."

"If I could do *that* and nothing else, you wouldn't be needed to pull the big guns at all. If I was like my captain – he can see things inside his head before the firing begins, and he shakes all over, but he knows too much to run away–if I was like him I could pull the guns. But if I were as wise as all that I should never be here. I should be a king in the forest, as I used to be, sleeping half the day and bathing when I liked. I haven't had a good bath for a month."

"That's all very fine," said Billy. "But giving a thing a long name doesn't make it any better."

"Hush!" said the troop horse. "I think I understand what Two Tails means."

"You'll understand better in a minute," said Two Tails angrily. "Now you just explain to me why you don't like this!"

He began trumpeting furiously at the top of his trumpet.

"Stop that!" said Billy and the troop horse

together, and I could hear them stamp and shiver. An elephant's trumpeting is always nasty, especially on a dark night.

"I shan't stop," said Two Tails. "Won't you explain that, please? *Hhrrmph! Rrrt! Rrrmph! Rrrhha!*" Then he stopped suddenly, and I heard a little whimper in the dark, and knew that Vixen had found me at last. She knew as well as I did that if there is one thing in the world the elephant is more afraid of than another it is a little barking dog. So she stopped to bully Two Tails in his pickets, and yapped round his big feet. Two Tails shuffled and squeaked. "Go away, little dog!" he said. "Don't snuff at my ankles, or I'll kick at you. Good little dog, nice little doggie, then! Go home, you yelping little beast! Oh, why doesn't someone take her away? She'll bite me in a minute."

"Seems to me," said Billy to the troop horse, "that our friend Two Tails is afraid of most things. Now, if I had a full meal for every dog I've kicked across the parade ground I should be as fat as Two Tails nearly."

I whistled, and Vixen ran up to me, muddy all over, and licked my nose, and told me a long tale about hunting for me all through the camp. I never let her know that I understood beast talk, or she would have taken all sorts of liberties. So I buttoned her into the breast of my overcoat, and Two Tails shuffled and stamped and growled to himself.

"Extraordinary! Most extraordinary!" he said. "It runs in our family. Now, where has that nasty little beast gone to?"

I heard him feeling about with his trunk.

"We all seem to be affected in various ways," he went on, blowing his nose. "Now, you gentlemen were alarmed, I believe, when I trumpeted."

"Not alarmed, exactly," said the troop horse, "but it made me feel as though I had hornets where my saddle ought to be. Don't begin again."

"I'm frightened of a little dog, and the camel here is frightened by bad dreams in the night."

"It is very lucky for us that we haven't all got to fight in the same way," said the troop horse.

"What I want to know," said the young mule, who had been quiet for a long time – "what I want to know is, why we have to fight at all."

"Because we're told to," said the troop horse,

with a snort of contempt.

"Orders," said Billy the mule, and his teeth snapped.

"*Hukm hai!*" (It is an order!), said the camel with a gurgle, and Two Tails and the bullocks repeated, "*Hukm hai!*"

"Yes, but who gives the orders?" said the recruit mule.

"The man who walks at your head – Or sits on your back – Or holds the nose rope – Or twists your tail," said Billy and the troop horse and the camel and the bullocks one after the other.

"But who gives them the orders?"

"Now you want to know too much, young un," said Billy, "and that is one way of getting kicked. All you have to do is to obey the man at your head and ask no questions."

"He's quite right," said Two Tails. "I can't always obey, because I'm betwixt and between. But Billy's right. Obey the man next to you who gives the order, or you'll stop all the battery, besides getting a thrashing."

The gun bullocks got up to go. "Morning is coming," they said. "We will go back to our lines.

It is true that we only see out of our eyes, and we are not very clever. But still, we are the only people tonight who have not been afraid. Good night, you brave people."

Nobody answered, and the troop horse said, to change the conversation, "Where's that little dog? A dog means a man somewhere about."

"Here I am," yapped Vixen, "under the gun tail with my man. You big, blundering beast of a camel you, you upset our tent. My man's very angry."

"*Phew!*" said the bullocks. "He must be white!"

"Of course he is," said Vixen. "Do you suppose I'm looked after by a bullock-driver?"

"*Huah! Ouach! Ugh!*" said the bullocks. "Let us get away quickly."

They plunged forward in the mud, and managed somehow to run their yoke on the pole of an ammunition wagon, where it jammed.

"Now you *have* done it," said Billy calmly. "Don't struggle. You're hung up till daylight. What on earth's the matter?"

The bullocks went off into the long hissing snorts that Indian cattle give, and pushed and crowded and slewed and stamped and slipped and nearly fell down in the mud, grunting savagely.

"You'll break your necks in a minute," said the troop horse. "What's the matter with white men? I live with 'em."

"They – eat – us! Pull!" said the near bullock. The yoke snapped with a twang, and they lumbered off together.

I never knew before what made Indian cattle so scared of Englishmen. We eat beef – a thing that no cattle driver touches – and of course the cattle do not like it.

"May I be flogged with my own pad-chains! Who'd have thought of two big lumps like those losing their heads?" said Billy.

"Never mind. I'm going to look at this man. Most of the white men, I know, have things in their pockets," said the troop horse.

"I'll leave you, then. I can't say I'm over-fond of 'em myself. Besides, white men who haven't a place to sleep in are more than likely to be thieves, and I've a good deal of Government property on my back. Come along, young un, and we'll go back to our lines. Good night, Australia! See you on parade tomorrow, I suppose. Good night, old Hay-bale! – try to control your feelings, won't you? Good night, Two Tails! If you pass us on the ground tomorrow, don't trumpet. It spoils our formation."

Billy the Mule stumped off with the swaggering limp of an old campaigner, as the troop horse's head came nuzzling into my breast, and I gave him biscuits, while Vixen, who is a most conceited little dog, told him fibs about the scores of horses that she and I kept.

"I'm coming to the parade tomorrow in my dog-cart," she said. "Where will you be?"

"On the left hand of the second squadron. I set the time for all my troop, little lady," he said politely. "Now I must go back to Dick. My tail's all muddy, and he'll have two hours' hard work dressing me for parade."

The big parade of all the thirty thousand men was held that afternoon, and Vixen and I had a good place close to the Viceroy and the Amir of Afghanistan, with his high big black hat of astrakhan wool and the great diamond star in the

centre. The first part of the review was all
sunshine, and the regiments went by in wave
upon wave of legs all moving together, and guns
all in a line, till our eyes grew dizzy. Then the
cavalry came up, to the beautiful cavalry canter
of "Bonnie Dundee," and Vixen cocked her ear
where she sat on the dog-cart. The second
squadron of the Lancers shot by, and there was
the troop horse, with his tail like spun silk, his
head pulled into his breast, one ear forward and
one back, setting the time for all his squadron, his
legs going as smoothly as waltz music. Then the
big guns came by, and I saw Two Tails and two
other elephants harnessed in line to a forty-
pounder siege gun, while twenty yoke of oxen
walked behind. The seventh pair had a new yoke,
and they looked rather stiff and tired. Last came
the screw guns, and Billy the mule carried
himself as though he commanded all the troops,
and his harness was oiled and polished till it
winked. I gave a cheer all by myself for Billy the
mule, but he never looked right or left.

The rain began to fall again, and for a while it
was too misty to see what the troops were doing.

They had made a big half circle across the plain, and were spreading out into a line. That line grew and grew and grew till it was three-quarters of a mile long from wing to wing – one solid wall of men, horses, and guns. Then it came on straight toward the Viceroy and the Amir, and as it got nearer the ground began to shake, like the deck of a steamer when the engines are going fast.

Unless you have been there you cannot imagine what a frightening effect this steady come-down of troops has on the spectators, even when they know it is only a review. I looked at the Amir. Up till then he had not shown the shadow of a sign of astonishment or anything else. But now his eyes began to get bigger and bigger, and he picked up the reins on his horse's neck and looked behind him. For a minute it seemed as though he were going to draw his sword and slash his way out through the English men and women in the carriages at the back. Then the advance stopped dead, the ground stood still, the whole line saluted, and thirty bands began to play all together. That was the end of the review, and the regiments went off to their

camps in the rain, and an infantry band struck
up with –

The animals went in two by two, Hurrah!
The animals went in two by two,
The elephant and the battery mul',
and they all got into the Ark
For to get out of the rain!

Then I heard an old grizzled, long-haired
Central Asian chief, who had come down with
the Amir, asking questions of a Indian officer.

"Now," said he, "in what manner was this
wonderful thing done?"

And the officer answered, "An order was given,
and they obeyed."

"But are the beasts as wise as the men?" said
the chief.

"They obey, as the men do. Mule, horse,
elephant, or bullock, he obeys his driver, and the
driver his sergeant, and the sergeant his
lieutenant, and the lieutenant his captain, and the
captain his major, and the major his colonel, and
the colonel his brigadier commanding three

regiments, and the brigadier the general, who obeys the Viceroy, who is the servant of the Empress. Thus it is done."

"Would it were so in Afghanistan!" said the chief, "for there we obey only our own wills."

"And for that reason," said the Indian officer, twirling his moustache, "your Amir whom you do not obey must come here and take orders from our Viceroy."

PARADE SONG OF THE CAMP ANIMALS

ELEPHANTS OF THE GUN TEAMS

We lent to Alexander the strength of Hercules,
The wisdom of our foreheads, the cunning of our knees;
We bowed our necks to service: they ne'er were loosed again, –
Make way there – way for the ten-foot teams
Of the Forty-Pounder train!

GUN BULLOCKS

Those heroes in their harnesses avoid a cannonball,
And what they know of powder upsets them one and all;
Then we come into action and tug the guns again –
Make way there – way for the twenty yoke
Of the Forty-Pounder train!

CAVALRY HORSES

By the brand on my shoulder, the finest of tunes
Is played by the Lancers, Hussars, and Dragoons,
And it's sweeter than "Stables" or "Water" to me –
The Cavalry Canter of "Bonnie Dundee"!

Then feed us and break us and handle and groom,
And give us good riders and plenty of room,
And launch us in column of squadron and see
The way of the war horse to "Bonnie Dundee"!

SCREW-GUN MULES

As me and my companions were scrambling up a hill,
The path was lost in rolling stones, but we went forward still;
For we can wriggle and climb, my lads,
and turn up everywhere,
Oh, it's our delight on a mountain height,
with a leg or two to spare!

Good luck to every sergeant, then, that lets us pick our road;
Bad luck to all the driver men that cannot pack a load:
For we can wriggle and climb, my lads,
and turn up everywhere,
Oh, it's our delight on a mountain height,
with a leg or two to spare!

COMMISSARIAT CAMELS

We haven't a camelty tune of our own
To help us trollop along,
But every neck is a hair trombone
(Rtt-ta-ta-ta! is a hair trombone!)
And this is our marching-song:
Can't! Don't! Shan't! Won't!
Pass it along the line!
Somebody's pack has slid from his back,
Wish it were only mine!
Somebody's load has tipped off in the road –
Cheer for a halt and a row!
Urrr! Yarrh! Grr! Arrh!
Somebody's catching it now!

ALL THE BEASTS TOGETHER
Children of the Camp are we,
Serving each in his degree;
Children of the yoke and goad,
Pack and harness, pad and load.
See our line across the plain,
Like a heel-rope bent again,
Reaching, writhing, rolling far,
Sweeping all away to war!
While the men that walk beside,
Dusty, silent, heavy-eyed,
Cannot tell why we or they
March and suffer day by day.
Children of the Camp are we,
Serving each in his degree;
Children of the yoke and goad,
Pack and harness, pad and load!

Beyond the Story

Who was Rudyard Kipling?

BORN in India in 1865, Kipling loved the country and was said to have spoken Hindustani before he learnt English. When he was six, his parents sent him to England for his health and education. He hated the time he spent there, and after finishing school he returned to India. There he learnt his trade as a writer, working on a newspaper. His first fiction works were short stories and poems about Indian life, which were an immediate success. Over his long life he also wrote children's books, novels, poetry, essays, and history books. Kipling refused to accept a knighthood but was the first English writer to win the Nobel prize for Literature. He died in Sussex in 1936.

Kipling sometimes signed his drawings with a large letter A inside an ark because when you say 'Ark A' aloud it sounds like his initials - RK.

Background and Setting

FIRST published in 1894, *The Jungle Book* was originally accompanied by illustrations by Kipling's father, and was an instant success. It has come to light recently that it was written for his eldest daughter.

The setting is mostly in the jungles in Central India, but Kipling probably used his experience of visiting a jungle in northern India, when he was twenty-two. He said that he put everything he had learnt, heard or dreamt about the jungle into the tales. In 1895 Kipling wrote a sequel, with five further Mowgli stories, called *The Second Jungle Book*. There have been many film adaptions, including Walt Disney's 1967 cartoon, which is very different to the book.

The first half of Mowgli's name should be pronounced to rhyme with 'cow'.

Life in Victorian India

WHEN Kipling published *The Jungle Book* most of India had been ruled by the British for around fifty years. It was governed by a group of British men including civil servants, politicians, magistrates, policemen and a large army, consisting of both British regiments and Indian regiments led by British officers. In 'Rikki-Tikki-Tavi', the father is an army officer.

The Army

The British Army in India learnt to use local animals such as camels to carry heavy loads, and elephants and bullocks to pull their guns. 'Her Majesty's Servants' is a vivid picture of a group of army animals discussing what scares them in battle.

Victorian India was often called 'the Jewel in the Crown' of Britain's overseas colonies.

The British Civilian

Alongside the official administration, many other British people went out to work in India – farmers to grow tea, teak, rubber and other crops; missionaries to try and convert Indian people to Christianity; teachers to run colleges. Women went out to nurse or teach, and to be with their husbands. Children stayed in India in their pre-school years, but were then sent back to the UK to stay with relatives. Wives stayed with their husbands and many children did not see their parents for years.

Freedom

India was determined to break free from British rule and Mahatma Ghandi, widely described now as 'the father of the nation' organised a campaign of peaceful resistance to try and bring it about. India gained independence shortly after the Second World War in 1947.

Mahatma is an Indian title meaning 'great soul.'

Ideas and Influences

Here are some of the key themes (ideas) that Kipling explores in his influential story, *The Jungle Book*.

Wolf Children

Some cultures believe that there have been instances of children being reared by wolves. An early version of the myth is the story of Romulus and Remus, the legendary founders of Rome. Many Indian stories refer to wolf children. Mowgli has to decide if he is human or animal and work out where he belongs: identity is one of the most important themes in the book.

Hard Work and Responsibility

Kipling was very interested in the idea of people finding their proper work and tackling it with all their might. Many of the stories in *The Jungle Book* are about animals or people learning their roles, from Rikki-tikki-tavi to little Toomai. His stories also show how important he believed it was for a society to have rules and order – the laws of the jungle are there to teach all animals discipline.

The *bandar-log* are despised because they have no self-control. In contrast, the animals in 'Her Majesty's Servants' can conquer their fears and do a good job because they are well trained. Another theme is that of being different, and the risk – and rewards – of being outcast. Kotick the white seal literally swims against the tide to find a new home for his people, even though by doing so he loses friends and position.

Mowgli and the Boy Scouts

Lord Baden-Powell was so impressed by *The Jungle Book* that he begged Kipling to let him use its themes in his new organisation, the Boy Scouts. Kipling didn't usually grant such permissions, but Baden-Powell was very insistent. When Baden-Powell went on to form a version of the Scouts for younger children, he called the boys Wolf Cubs, and their leader Akela.

About the Animals

KIPLING cleverly incorporated well-observed qualities of real life animals into his characters.

Mongooses such as Rikki-tikki-tavi were indeed kept as pets in India. They are curious creatures, known to often attack and kill snakes, as described in the story.

Kotick, the white seal, is a rare Northern Fur seal, a species that historically has been much hunted for its fur.

The Indian elephant, which features in 'Little Toomai' and 'Her Majesty's Servants', is smaller than the African elephant and can be trained to work. There are still many elephants working in India, to shift logs and as transport.

Baloo, "the sleepy brown bear who teaches the wolf cubs the Law of the Jungle," is probably a Sloth bear – this species inhabits the Seoni hills where the story is set.

Although the wolves in *The Jungle Book* are described as grey, the Indian wolf actually has a reddish tinge to its fur.

Bagheera is a panther – a black type of Indian leopard. Despite his dark, inky colouring, he still has patterned fur.

Kaa, the powerful snake, is a rock python, but his size is exaggerated – the longest recorded Indian Rock python was 4.9 metres in length.

Quick Quiz

Test how well you know the stories of *The Jungle Book*! You can find the answers on page 320.

1. What kind of animal is Mang in the story?

2. What does Mowgli's wolf mother's name mean?

3. What do the jungle animals call fire?

4. What are the master words of the hunting people?

5. What insult does Kotick shout at the Sea-Vitch?

6. What one word sums up the Law of the Jungle?

7. Where does the snake Nagaina lay her eggs?

8. How old is Little Toomai?

9. Where does the troop-horse come from?

10. What is the name of the narrator's dog in 'Her Majesty's Servants'?

Write Your Own Adventure

If you've been inspired by Rudyard Kipling's writing, here are some ideas to get you started with your own.

· There are many stories of children being raised by animals. Explore what it would be like to be brought up by a different species to wolves.

· An animal's quest for a safe home often describes a long journey. *Watership Down* by Richard Adams is a story showing rabbits going on a similar quest to Kotick's. Can you create your own version?

· Imagine Rikki-tikki-tavi's story as if it were told from the point of view of Darzee's wife. Start by giving her a name.

· Imagine you are the female seal who decided to wait for Kotick to return. It may have taken a different kind of bravery for her to not lose faith that he would return when her friends were starting families.

About the Artist

ESTER García Cortés was born in Cáceres, Spain, in 1984. For as long as she can remember, she has loved colour pencils, acrylics and pastels. After graduating in Fine Arts at the University of Salamanca in Spain, she moved to the city of Madrid. Here she started working in publishing houses, dedicating herself totally to her dream of being an artist.

Today, Ester works in pencil, watercolour, acrylic and also digitally. She is always searching for a way to express her thoughts through her illustrations, and so her rich, atmospheric style perfectly suits Kipling's imaginative world of *The Jungle Book*.

Answers:
1. A bat 2. 'Demon' 3. The Red Flower 4. 'We be of one blood, you and I.' 5. 'Clam-eater.' 6. 'Obey.' 7. In the melon bed 8. Ten years old 9. Australia 10. Vixen